Wrote
for Luck

Stories

Also By D.J. Taylor

FICTION

Great Eastern Land
Real Life
English Settlement
After Bathing at Baxter's: Stories
Trespass
The Comedy Man
Kept: A Victorian Mystery
Ask Alice
At the Chime of a City Clock
Derby Day
Secondhand Daylight
The Windsor Faction
From the Heart

NON-FICTION

A Vain Conceit: British Fiction in the 1980s
Other People: Portraits from the '90s (with Marcus Berkmann)
After the War: The Novel and England since 1945
Thackeray
Orwell: The Life
On the Corinthian Spirit: The Decline of Amateurism and Sport
Bright Young People: The Rise and Fall of a Generation 1918-1940
What You Didn't Miss: A Book of Literary Parodies

Wrote
for Luck

 *Stories*

D.J. TAYLOR

GALLEY BEGGAR PRESS

The right of D.J. Taylor to be identified as
the author of this work has been asserted
by him in accordance with the Copyright,
Designs and Patents Act, 1988

The Acknowledgements on page 205 constitute
an extension of this copyright page

A CIP record for this book is available
from the British Library

ISBN 978-1-910296-26-4

Text designed and typeset by Tetragon, London

Printed in Great Britain by Clays Ltd, St Ives plc

Contents

Leo's

Some
Versions
of Pastoral

T he flowers in the Underwoods' garden were all in bright, primary colours: yellows, blues and reds in charmless profusion. To negotiate them was to pass through the pages of a children's picture book where all the animals had grown to fantastic sizes and nuance was forever kept at bay. Somewhere near at hand invisible insects buzzed ominously and there was a smell of aftershave. Further away, screened by giant hedges, to which an amateur topiarist had done untold damage, they could hear some animal or person thrashing about in the undergrowth. Buzz of bees; sickly scent; odd, chirruping noises deep in the foliage: the surprisingly sinister spell cast by these phenomena was suddenly broken by the sound of Mr Underwood's voice – high, querulous and apparently belonging neither to man or woman – bursting through the verdure.

'Hi! Over here! Through the gap in the bank. You know the way.'

They found the gap in the bank, which was more of a declivity caused by the earth falling away from the stumps of a couple of beech trees, and came tumbling out onto a square of emerald grass so scrupulously cut that it might have been manicured. Here other hedges rose on three sides to a height of eight or nine feet. There was no escape, either from the semi-circle of garden chairs, the occasional table spread with tea-things, or

Mr and Mrs Underwood, who, proud and statuesque, like the elders of some benighted South American tribe, finally discovered in their Amazonian bolt-hole, sat waiting to receive them.

'I suppose you had trouble in parking your car on the green,' Mrs Underwood said, in a voice surprisingly like her husband's. Tony looked at his watch and found that they were only three minutes late. 'It does get rather clogged up at this time of year, what with all the *trippers* visiting the hall. There was a dreadful ice-cream van used to come and set up there,' Mrs Underwood went on, 'jangling its bell until all hours and making the air hideous, but Bunny got onto the parish council and put a stop to it.'

'How dreadful for you to be inconvenienced like that,' Jane said, who was less in awe of the Underwoods than her husband and could not resist teasing them when the opportunity presented itself.

How old were the Underwoods, Tony wondered, taking a closer look at the pair of cashmere-clad manikins, each with the same ley-lined faces and sun-cured skin, bolt upright in their chairs. Eighty? Eighty-five? And how long had he and Jane been visiting them? Twenty-five years? Thirty? All this time along the track he could not even recall their original connection with the Underwoods or what impulse continued to send them, annually, and with varying degrees of enthusiasm, to a part of Suffolk where the A-roads gave out, the sat-nav was cowed into incoherence and even the locals could not be relied upon for directions.

'We were listening to a programme about Patrick Leigh Fermor on the wireless,' Mrs Underwood said – her forename was either Oenone, or Christabel, he could never remember which – pronouncing Leigh Fermor's name in a way that was new to him and pushing a tea-cup towards him, inch by inch, over the white-clothed table-top. 'Now, you will be very careful of this, won't you?'

What heights had the tea-cup scaled in its past life that such efforts had to be made to preserve it? Done service on some far-off Garsington lawn? Been sipped out of by one of the Bloomsbury Group? There were pictures of Virginia Woolf and Carrington on the wall of the Underwoods' tiny drawing-room, and a bookcase harbouring the signed first editions of Cyril Connolly and Angus Wilson. It was a thoroughly innocuous piece of china, blue-and-white-striped, of a kind that you saw displayed in every roadside pottery the length and breadth of Cornwall, but nevertheless he brought his lips gratefully against its rim. The tea was Lapsang Souchong and rank as a civet, like ogres' perfume.

'I'm very fortunate to be able to welcome you at all,' Mrs Underwood said, in an impossibly queenly way. 'Why, this morning, taking the post in from the postman – such a nice man, but he will leave the parcels at the back door – I practically came a *cropper* on the step.'

Trippers. Wirelesses. Coming a cropper. There was a defiance about the manner in which Mrs Underwood dealt out these archaisms. The times had changed, but she would not. The reek of the aftershave turned out to come from her husband. Perhaps Mr Underwood was not quite such a barnacled adherent to the hull of the old world as his wife. Who could tell? The box hedges that surrounded them on three sides were quite impenetrable. Anything could have been concealed behind them: bare, empty plains; marauding armies; a hunt in wild halloo. Here in the Underwoods' Suffolk garden they were cut off, surrounded, as detached as any plant in its pot.

'The children send their...' – he was going to say 'love', but then compromised on 'best wishes.' This was a lie. The children had long ago baulked at any amenities offered by the Underwoods. But he was more worried by the blue-and-white cup, Virginia's nosegay, the repository of Cyril Connolly's night-cap, or whatever it had done, which, like most other sanctified artefacts, had twice nearly bobbed out of his hand and had to be set down with a rattle and a slight spillage of tea on the table-top.

'Daddy used to say,' Mrs Underwood now volunteered, with what might have been an attempt at humour, 'that children were a necessary affliction. Of course, Bunny and I never saw the need for them ourselves.'

A gust of wind, all unheralded, came dipping over the tops of the box-hedges and blew up one of the fronds of Mr Underwood's sparse, elf-white hair into a kind of quiff. As generally happened on these afternoons in Suffolk, with the Lapsang Souchong pungently abrew and the starlings racketing in the thickets, there came a moment when the jigsaw of their association fell neatly into place and he remembered, first, that Mrs Underwood's father had been a literary man of the inter-war era whose diaries had been the subject of a contemptuous review in the *Sunday Times*, and, second, that Mr Underwood had been a director of the gentlemanly (and now defunct) publishing firm for which, a quarter of a century ago, Jane had served out her apprenticeship as a secretary-typist.

There was another odd thing about Mr Underwood, Tony noticed, in addition to the reek of aftershave. He was wearing round his withered neck a small but punctiliously constructed daisy chain. There was something faintly macabre about this, as if he was about to take part in a pagan ritual, or the tea-cup, caught beneath his long, spatulate fingers, was brimful of virgins' blood.

'How is your book going?' Jane asked, who tabled this question every time they came to the Underwoods and had once been rewarded with a story of how Evelyn Waugh had got stuck in the lavatory at a publishers' lunch.

'Yes, how is your book going?' he joined in, thinking that such straws as these were there to be clutched at. But there were no more stories about Evelyn Waugh and defective door-keys, faint cries of abandonment echoing in far-off corridors, merely the sense of a painful subject recklessly disinterred by people who should have known better.

'Oh, I've given it up,' Bunny said, with a little cackle of disdain. Tony, who had been trying for some time to work out what he reminded him of, realised that it was a photograph of the aged Somerset Maugham shortly after his first injection of monkey-glands. 'I decided that there are far too many books in the world already. Heaven knows, I was responsible for hundreds of them myself. And then I don't think anybody is really interested in Cyril these days.'

'Of course, you know Bunny did nearly everything for Cyril towards the end,' Mrs Underwood said loyally. 'Got all those first editions sold for him at Sotheby's. Published that collection of *belles lettres* for him when no one else would take it on. There was even some talk of his being appointed literary executor. And then when that dreadful man came to write the biography, there was hardly any mention of him at all.'

This was true, but it prompted other questions, mostly unanswerable. Could you rate your life on the number of index references you achieved in a biography of Cyril Connolly? Or the celebrated mouths that had bent to drink out of one of your tea-cups seventy years ago? Mr Underwood looked as if he were going to sat something else about his memoirs, whose provisional title, Tony now recalled, had been *Dawn in Wardour Street*, and then thought better of it. The breeze was still swerving in over the box hedges and sending little fragments of wood-chip cartwheeling over the virid grass.

'Did you see the documentary about Benjamin Britten on BBC Four the other day?' Jane asked bravely. 'There were some very nice shots of Aldeburgh.'

But the Underwoods had not seen the programme about Benjamin Britten. Neither had they heard of the Corot exhibition at the Tate of whose contents Jane now gamely offered details. Each year the range of their cultural interests shrank a little further while their disapproval of the life lived out beyond their Suffolk fastness increased. This did not make conversation easy, a fact that Mrs Underwood, to do her justice, seemed to appreciate.

'Of course, we are dreadful recluses,' she said at one point. 'But then, we did our share of gadding about the world in our day, and one can't keep up that kind of thing forever.'

Downwind of the Lapsang Souchong the smell was not so bad. What kind of gadding about had the Underwoods done in their day, he wondered? P&O cruises to locations filched from the *National Geographic?* Visits to the stately homes whose owners' reminiscences Mr Underwood had schemed so valiantly to publish? And now here they were in a Suffolk garden, beaten back by time, with the world they knew sunk beneath the encroaching tide. He tried Bunny with a book about Kingsley Amis he had seen reviewed in one of the Sundays and got nowhere. Mrs Underwood, rising to her feet to inspect the tea-pot, looked suddenly shrunken, impossibly diminutive. She could not have been more than four feet ten. Not only had time beaten the Underwoods back; it had made them smaller. Soon at this rate they would vanish altogether.

'Time for a refill,' Mrs Underwood said, with what could have been deep-seated resentment or the placid acceptance of pleasure to come. It was inconceivable that so frail a piece of humanity should be able to lift the tea-things, so, tray in hand, he tracked her back through the verdant labyrinths and across a lawn where rooks grimly disputed cast-off bacon-rinds to a cubby-hole of a kitchen, where tea towels hung up to dry in the sun and the thought of being in a Beatrix Potter story where Johnny Town Mouse might soon appear at the window with his tail twirled over his top-coated arm was rather too strong for comfort. Here, framed in the triangle made by a Welsh dresser, a sink piled high with earthenware plates and an empty bird-cage suspended from wood-wormed rafters, Mrs Underwood turned unexpectedly resolute.

'Of course Bunny's not himself,' she said, filling the tea-kettle with several badly-aimed spurts of water from the tap. 'Not in the least. I don't know what's the matter with him. It may be medical. It may be not. There are some mornings when he won't get out of bed at all. The other day I found him writing a letter – *writing a letter* – to some actress he'd seen on the television.'

There was something horribly symbolic about the bird-cage with its gilded bars and open door. What had lived in there? What had caused it to take flight?

'What sort of a letter?' Tony wondered. After all, the actress could have been Judi Dench or Eileen Atkins.

'An extraordinarily embarrassing one,' Mrs Underwood said, without turning a hair. 'Quite out of the question that it should be sent. I told him I would take it to the post, but after he'd given it to me I simply took it into the study and tore it into pieces. It's no end to a life, you know. Not for either of us.'

In all the years that they had been coming to Kersey, all the years that they had splashed through minor rivers that ran over village pavements, looked for road signs lost in the spreading hedgerows and sat pacifically behind items of slow-moving agricultural machinery, Mrs Underwood had never grown confidential. This was such an awful conceptualisation of her plight that he felt he had to say something.

'You mustn't think that,' he volunteered. 'I'm sure you must have a great deal to comfort yourselves with. 'I mean…' – he tried to think of something with which the Underwoods could comfort themselves – 'I mean, there's all the fine work that Bunny did… Your father.'

'Bunny's *work*,' Mrs Underwood said, and left it at that. There was not enough room in the kitchen, and the job of unloading the first batch of tea-things onto the draining board was made more difficult by the curiously jerky movements – like some marionette whose strings were twisted from on high – that Mrs Underwood made as she spoke.

'As for my father's diaries,' she went on emphatically, 'do you know, there was a whole section – twenty thousand words at least – that I made the man strike out? It was all about when I was at school and how spotty I was, and not beautiful, and what a disappointment I was to him. I can't tell you,' Mrs Underwood said, drawing herself up to her full height and suddenly seeming taller, vastier and more consequential than she had ever done before, 'how much it upset me. I minded most frightfully… Oh, for goodness sake, be *careful!*'

But it was too late. The blue-and-white china cup had rolled away from his imploring grasp and smashed into fragments on the red-stone floor. Mrs Underwood bent to retrieve them, and having done so stood sorrowfully with them in the palm of her out-stretched hand, like a votive offering brought to the shrine of some pagan god.

'Lytton's cup,' she said miserably. 'Lytton's cup.' Outside the noise of the rooks, still grimly disputing their bacon-rinds, rose to frenzy, followed by a human cry, so wild and alarming that they rushed into the garden to see who had made it. Here they were able to contemplate the interesting spectacle of an upturned easy chair, a second, shattered tea-cup and Mr Underwood, on hands and knees, daisy chain all askew, struggling to right himself. Jane stood at his side, a bit uncertainly, like a schoolmistress whose favourite pupil has cried off sick ten minutes into an exam, the expression on her face half mild amusement and half genuine alarm.

Half-an-hour later, in the car driving west through the Suffolk back-lanes, past the head-high clumps of cow-parsley and the loosestrife-patterned hedges, he said: 'I don't believe for a moment it was Lytton Strachey's tea-cup.'

'It could quite easily have been when you come to think about it.'

'Well, they ought to have kept it locked up in a cupboard then, or given it to a museum, where passing chartered accountants couldn't get at it.' Mrs Underwood had not said anything as she consigned the shards of china to the waste-paper basket. In some ways this cut deeper than the sharpest rebuke. Something else struck him and he said:

'I know what you said to Oenone... to Christabel about the chair giving way, but why exactly did Bunny end up on the grass?'

'I told you. He asked me, quite conversationally, as if he wanted me to pass the rock-buns, if I would come and "live with him and be his love". Those were his exact words.'

'And what did you do?'

'I told him not to be so silly.'

'Then what happened?'

'There was a bit of scuffling. And after that, because I was rather cross and I don't like people's fingers digging into my hand, I just gave him a tiny push.'

The road signs, which had hitherto been sporadic and confusing, now suggested that they were somewhere near Colchester. He thought of Bunny's balding, aftershave-scented head waggling above its necklace of daisies, and then of Mrs Underwood explaining how frightfully she had minded about her father's diaries. His own father had kept a diary in which he had recorded the price of petrol and the avian traffic of their south-west London back-garden. There had been nothing in it of a personal nature, and no spotty daughters. Whatever pained disappointment he might have felt had been kept to himself.

'Do you know,' she said. 'Somebody told me that she once had an affair with Philip Larkin?'

'Well I hope they both enjoyed themselves. And that he had a light hand with the crockery.'

He found himself imagining Oenone or Christabel sitting in a restaurant with Philip Larkin. The scene had a tuppence-coloured air of unreality. They were on the motorway now, flanked by a throng of mobile homes and caravans making their way back from the coast. Somewhere in the world, he supposed, lurked an art which you could set against the armies of commerce and bureaucracy to lay them waste, but it could not be found in the Underwoods' green-girt garden. They set off home through the concrete and steel, past shoals of cars from which pale, incurious faces stared out, a firmament where broken cups were of little account and nobody, whether in jest or earnest, asked anyone to live with them and be their love.

—2013

Jermyn
Street

'**N**ot much of a job is it?' the barmaid wondered. 'That depends,' Sinclair said. 'You'd be surprised who comes in there sometimes.'

'Who does? What sort of people?'

Sinclair changed tack. 'I sold a chair last week cost five hundred pounds.'

It was still early in the pub and no one much was about. In the corner of the front bar the two men who worked in the shipping office were having one of their conversations that Sinclair could never understand, however much he eavesdropped. The smoke from their cigarettes undulated in folds through the stale air. Outside the February slush was turning grey-brown at the edges.

'Funny hours you work anyway,' the barmaid said.

'I come and go,' Sinclair told her. He moved to one side as a small, white-faced man he didn't recognise advanced on the bar, wondering what to do. Mr Savage liked him to have a 'good long lunch-hour', as he put it, but it was cold out, he didn't fancy a hot meal in the pub, and he badly wanted to be back in the shop. When the barmaid had finished serving the small man he bought a Scotch egg and a pork pie from one of the glass display cases – curtly, as if to emphasise that the intimacy of a minute ago didn't really count for anything – took them down to St James's Square and ate them standing underneath a tree in the gardens as melting snow dripped down on him from the upper branches. Crossing the broad sweep of the square's corner on the way back to the shop a skidding cyclist brushed against his coat and he shouted a warning, hoping that the man would shout back, but he was already away in the direction of Regent Street.

Back at the shop Mr Savage was haggling with a customer over a set of carved ivory chessmen. Neither of them looked up as he came in, jangling the shop bell violently. Sinclair went into the room at the back, took off his coat and began to fill the electric kettle at the sink. Another pile of books had arrived on the scratched deal table in his absence and he looked along their spines as he made the coffee. *Ladslove Lyrics. A Coan Anthology. A History of the Boy.* People would sometimes pay as much as fifty pounds for a book of this kind, Sinclair knew. Holding the coffee mugs carefully at arm's length, he walked back into the shop. Mr Savage stood on his own, staring regretfully at the chess set. Sinclair put the mugs down sharply on the glass counter next to a faded print of the Tower of London and a Victorian miniature of a girl playing a mandolin.

'Didn't you sell it?' he asked.

Mr Savage made an apologetic little bob of his head. 'Not a serious customer.' Mr Savage always said this when a deal fell through.

Sinclair shrugged. 'That stuff won't sell itself,' he said reproachfully.

Six months ago, when he'd taken the job, he would have been amazed if anyone had told him he'd end up talking to

Mr Savage like this. The odd thing was that Mr Savage didn't seem to mind. He reminded Sinclair of a boy he'd known at school, a weak little white-haired kid called Damian who for some reason didn't care if you threw his bag in the road or ran into him, and even seemed to get a kick out of your hostility.

Outside expensively shod feet pittered up and down the arcade's marble floor. Another customer came into the shop and started riffling aimlessly through the tray of prints. Mr Savage watched him, taking quick, nervous sips from his coffee cup. There was something worrying him, Sinclair could see. The man who had been looking at the tray of prints eventually paid twenty pounds for a representation of Putney Bridge executed in 1827: about twice what it was worth, Sinclair calculated. Mr Savage smoothed the two ten-pound notes between his fingers of one hand and used the other to stroke his thin, greying hair into place.

'I was wondering if you had anything special planned for this afternoon, Neville. For the shop, I mean.'

Sinclair thought rapidly. Usually he spent afternoons in the basement storeroom sorting through the unsold stock or effecting minor repairs to items Mr Savage thought needed 'improving'.

'That depends, doesn't it?'

'Only there were one or two...' Mr Savage stopped the sentence halfway through and stared awkwardly at the coffee cup he was twisting between his fingers. For a second Sinclair realised that he almost felt sorry for him, having to sell books like *A History of the Boy* for a living to snooty American tourists, not to mention the rows with Anthea or whatever her name was. But he wasn't going to help Mr Savage out of his embarrassment. Or not quite yet.

'And then when my wife gets here—'

'You want me to go up to Camden Market. I could probably manage it,' Sinclair said, trying to sound a good deal more aggrieved than he actually felt.

Mr Savage smiled. He put his hand gingerly on Sinclair's forearm and moved the fingers up and down. 'Thank you, Neville,' he said sincerely. 'I appreciate that.'

For some reason the shop was always quiet after lunch. Outside in the arcade the swirl of midday traffic had given way to occasional solitary women who stared vaguely at Mr Savage through the plate glass and then went away again. The doorbell hadn't rung for half an hour. In the basement Sinclair applied varnish strenuously to the legs of a 'gout stool', which was Mr Savage's usual description of any small chair made before the year 1900. As soon as Anthea got there he knew he would have to leave for Camden, maybe even before. It was always worse in the shop immediately after she had arrived. Sometimes he wondered what the effect of having him there had on the two of them, whether they liked having him as an audience or whether they were as disconcerted as he was. You could never tell with people like the Savages.

Anthea came at ten past three. Sinclair gave her a couple of minutes, then left in a hurry, shouldering his way through the empty air with a 'Bye' flung in the direction of the till. Looking back through the window he could see the Savages turning towards each other and the little 'o' of Mrs Savage's mouth as she started speaking again. Along Piccadilly the wind had got up and he hunched his jacket over his chest as he made for the tube. A woman swerved slightly to avoid his onward rush and Sinclair glared at her. The tube was almost empty. Glancing over the advertisements for foreign holidays and mobile phones, Sinclair found himself thinking about the shop and what someone like Mr Savage did with his spare time. Films, maybe? TV? That set him on the other familiar train of thought, back to the hostel and the big TV screen they had there and the old man, McKechnie, falling asleep in his chair while the others watched films and drank cans of stout into the small hours.

At Camden Town it had started to rain and there were tiny streaks of water slanting across the windows of Jellaby's shop. Two of the panes had been replaced by squares of brown paper criss-crossed with Sellotape, Sinclair noticed. He found Mr Jellaby in the front, hands in pockets, surrounded by piles of old magazines. 'Bloody kids,' he said as Sinclair came in, gesturing sharply at the window. Sinclair stared at the topmost magazine, which was a 1969 copy of the *National Geographic.* 'Kids do that?' he asked, knowing that talking to Mr Jellaby was preferable to the icy silence of not talking to him.

'Who else?' Mr Jellaby wondered, less crossly. He was a small, fantastically dirty man in his fifties. Sinclair had never once seen anyone else in his shop, not even one of the dossers from the market trying to part-exchange books.' What you got then?'Mr Jellaby went on. Sinclair gave him the brown envelope that Mr Savage always left in the little aperture

under the till. He was tired now, he realised. What he really
fancied was a nap in the Savages' basement. Perhaps he'd
get one later, unless Anthea was still poking around there.
'Stay here a bit, will you?' Mr Jellaby said. Sinclair watched
him shuffle off towards the back of the shop, where there
were a couple of huge porphyry vases and a yellow curtain
that blocked off Mr Jellaby's living quarters. Somewhere in
the distance a phone rang and he heard Mr Jellaby talking
into it, so softly that his voice barely broke over the noise of
the rain. Sinclair sat down in a wrecked armchair next to the
nearest pile of magazines. He was so tired that he wanted to
sleep, but the thought of Mr Jellaby standing over him, maybe
even shaking his shoulder to wake him, made him stand up
again and light a cigarette. He'd smoked three-quarters of it
by the time Mr Jellaby came back. 'Fags is it?' he said. 'Want
a cup of tea or something?' Sinclair shook his head. One
day he'd really get talking to Mr Jellaby, he thought, really
draw him out, but not now, not in the empty shop with the
water running down the window, hemmed in by the piles of
magazines. He wedged the Jiffy bag Mr Jellaby had given him
under one arm and stubbed the cigarette out on the sole of
his boot. 'That's right,' Mr Jellaby said approvingly. 'Saves on
the bloody mess too.'

There were magazines in the Jiffy bag, Sinclair knew.
Much worse than anything Mr Savage sold in the shop. Once
he'd taken one out on the tube and looked at it, and then
put it away because he realised everyone was looking at him.
Coming back along Piccadilly he had the queer feeling that
the people who passed him knew what he was carrying. This

made him quicken his step and he took the last few yards down the arcade at a run, so that the shop windows were a blur of light and colour and he nearly fell over a can that someone had left in a doorway. In the shop Mr and Mrs Savage were standing on each side of the counter making extravagant gestures at each other – weird hailings and flourishes like a page of semaphore instructions Sinclair had once seen in a book. From the look on their faces they'd been at it ever since he'd left. He came into the room with a deliberate nonchalance, just to show Anthea that he wasn't afraid of her or anything, and stood carelessly by the till until they stopped bickering. In the end there was a silence and he looked at them – Mrs Savage red and furious, Mr Savage sad but somehow stubbornly refusing to give way. 'Been enjoying yourselves?' he asked. He knew it would only annoy Mrs Savage more, but he couldn't stop himself.

Mrs Savage sucked in her breath. 'And as for him,' she said, picking up an old grievance, 'I don't know how you can bear to look at him, I just don't.' Sinclair ignored her. Looking at Mr Savage's pasty, put-upon face, he thought suddenly of Damian, the kid at school, remembered pushing his elbow into his face once and the glance Damian gave him: half woeful, half expectant. Suddenly he became aware that the three of them were doing a kind of dance, he and Mr Savage crossing and re-crossing the room to avoid the sweeps of Mrs Savage's arm. Mr Savage began to say, 'I think, Neville…' but something in Sinclair broke and he pushed the Jiffy bag urgently towards him. 'Here,' he said, 'these are for you.' Together they watched the glistening pages drop out of the bag's gaping neck, tumble to the floor and split apart, a piece of frozen time made up of cheap, shiny paper, Mrs Savage's tiny scream, the memory of the elbow ramming home, that for some reason he would always remember.

—1999

As Long
As He Lies
Perfectly Still

Towards dawn what might have been a child's cry rose from behind the eighth-open door that divided the two rooms of their 'family suite' – lost and indistinct but somehow eldritch, faintly inhuman in its register – and she raised herself up on one elbow, eyes straining through the murk, waiting for the flurry of purposeful movement, the small head framed in the oblong of stark light, caught irresolutely between door and jamb. But the cry faded away, leaving her stranded and inert, with only the sound of Jamie breathing heavily into his pillow and the patter of the travelling alarm clock to break the silence. It was 5am, but not, Claire thought, quite as cold as it might have been. Still oppressed by the various neuroses she had taken to bed with her six hours before, she got up and twitched open the curtain to reveal the Holiday Inn forecourt in all its neon-tinted glory, like a sci-fi film set dropped arbitrarily onto the Oxfordshire verdure.

Even at 5am there were people about, goading cars noisily out of their parking bays, smoking cigarettes down by the breeze-blocked foyer. Why did people have to get up at five on a Sunday morning, she wondered, much less smoke cigarettes against the dawn? There was a copy of the book lying on the upturned suitcase, the pages separated into quarter-inch clumps by a line of book-marks and Post-it notes, left there expressly to intoxicate, even now, before daylight in an Oxford hotel room, quite irresistible. Waking an hour later to visit the bathroom, Jamie found her perched with it on the lavatory seat, altogether lost in this newly minted despatch from the tumbling world of her imagination. 'You don't have to have it by heart, you know,' he said. 'I mean, you're only supposed to read from it.' There were real cries coming from the farther room, emphatically human. 'Your public awaits,' Jamie said.

At breakfast, while the children exclaimed over plates of food which they did not in the end eat, they reviewed the engagements that lay before them.

'You won't want the kids with you in the tent, I mean,' Jamie said. On the hotel forecourt, beyond the window, the cigarette smokers had given way to wary Asian taxi-drivers. 'So they'd better come to Merton with me.'

A bright new blob of colour had suddenly emerged into the mosaic of the day. 'Why exactly is it you have to go to Merton anyway?'

'There's that conference coming up in the autumn at Leicester, and Roger thought...'

Claire could never remember whether Roger was the one cheated out of his professorship by a conniving vice-chancellor or the one whose wife had left him, or which in Jamie's scale of values would be the deeper hurt. She applied herself to the tomatoes on her plate while Jamie's voice, lost for a second or two against the buzz and clamour of the meal, came halt-ingly back into focus.

'...And then you could get down to meet us at the res-taurant at 12.30.'

The children's antennae, indifferent to talk of Roger, conferences at Leicester or what Mummy might be doing in a tent, were finely tuned to the mention of restaurants. 'Who's going to be there?' Lucy wondered. 'Daddy's friends Hugo and Anna.' As she said the words she delved into her bag again and felt the book's spine resting against her thumb.

There was a silence. 'But we saw them last time we came here,' Jack said. 'And Tom's weird.'

It was true, Claire acknowledged to herself, pushing the uneaten tomatoes to the edge of her plate. They had seen Hugo and Anna last time they came here. And Tom was weird. But friendships, Jamie's friendships, took no account of repetition or incremental oddity.

'Well, it will be nice to see them again,' she found herself saying, to no one in particular. 'And now Mummy has to go.'

'If they've got that new thing about the Norman succession in the shop you might get it for me,' Jamie said. He was paler than usual, Claire noted, and massaging his forehead in a way that portended trouble.

'I'll see if it's there. Are you starting a headache?'

'It's OK... The TV series was hopeless, but I've heard him lecture. Oh, and good luck.'

She smiled gratefully at him and then finally was gone, by Asian taxi-driver down the grey expanse of the Woodstock Road, then on foot through streets laden with memories, from which, rather to her surprise, she found that she quailed: a shop from which she had walked, quite unthinkingly, without paying for a copy of Keith Thomas's *Man and the Natural World*, a pedestrian crossing where she had once watched an old man fall dead from his bicycle, a seminar room jutting out over the High Street where, 20 years ago she now remembered, she had first set eyes on the tall, abstracted figure that was Jamie's younger self.

In the tent her voice seemed to fly away from her, go soaring off into the wide space beneath the canvas awning and hung there, with occasional downward swoops to menace the up-turned heads of the crowd. The audience did not seem put out by this dislocation. In the front row a goggle-eyed old lady stared at her so blindly that she might have been unconscious. At her side a grey-haired man in a cagoule took notes. Their questions were horribly familiar. Did Claire know that the town of Uttoxeter was very much not as she had described it? Was writing a novel difficult? What advice would she give to anyone so engaged? Afterwards she wrote 'With best wishes from Claire Jackson' on the title page of each of the five books held out for her inspection, gave her email address to the intent-looking woman who proposed to send her 'a manuscript written by my friend who sadly couldn't be here' and strode out again into the college quadrangle, simultaneously exalted and cast down. The manuscript would lie unread on the dining-room table for a month and then be courteously returned, Claire knew. She had reached the door of the restaurant in Little Clarendon Street – gentrified now, and free of the student hordes – before she remembered Hugo and Anna, but there they were, a pair of smaller heads between them, ranged around the further side of a table that also harboured James and her own children: Hugo, who had written, ten years ago, a book called *The Saxon Hegemony*, and Anna, who laboured in a branch of intellectual copyright so abstruse that Claire had never been able to work out exactly what she did. Moving into the restaurant's dark interior, where Italianate waiters swam and glided, Claire was able to establish that Jamie, though paler still, was enjoying himself, and to suspect that some incidental trauma had disturbed the early stages of the meal. Seating herself between the children, she attended to the rush of whispered confidences.

'Mummy. Anna said the soup was horrible and she told the man to take it away.'

'Mummy. Tom's weirder than ever.'

On the pretext of examining the menu Claire took a look at Tom who, with Anna's arm protectively, or even janitorially, around his shoulders, was staring at a plate of pasta that someone – presumably not the chef – had cut into myriad tiny fragments. He scowled guilelessly back. Claire had never known how to deal with children like Tom. Either you conciliated them and they took advantage, or you stood no nonsense and suffered pangs of conscience in return. A sentence from one of Jamie's typescript piles, dumped on the bedside table a week ago, was coursing through her head: one may regard the relation between an Angevin suzcrain and his subject as a metaphor for the relation between imagination and its orchestrator. 'We were so sorry not to get to your reading,' Anna said, in that high, cracking voice which always made her sound as if she was on the edge of hysteria, 'but it was Emily's eurythmy class and then Sunday morning after that is Hugo's quiet time, when he…'

Whatever Hugo did – prune aspidistras or embroider antimacassars – ran away into a thicket of infant clamour and descending cutlery. She was a dark, intense girl with a long nose who had once confided to Claire that Tom was possibly not her child, and then forgotten it, leaving their conversations stuck in semi-intimacy, the planks beneath them sharply exposed, revealing dark, jagged rocks in the depths below. 'Did it, I mean, did it go OK?' Claire smiled appealingly at the waiter who seemed least offended by whatever humiliations had been piled upon him in the preceding half-hour and ordered an omelette, checked that her own children had not gone hungry (this had happened before) and realigned herself to the adult duologue going on at the end of the table.

Usually Jamie and Hugo discussed academic preferment, an extraordinary kind of three-dimensional chess, in which every move seemed to be cancelled out by developments on another plane. Just now, though, they were talking about what sounded like medieval kingship. Claire was pretty sure that she heard the words 'Plantagenet paradigm'. For a moment or so the half-chapter she had read in the tent at Christchurch, about sweet Izzy the public relations executive, her two-timing boyfriend and their too-small house in Wandsworth – not unlike her own too-small house in Wandsworth if it came to that – burned trails of shame through her memory, only for the sight of Hugo, gesturing lavishly with a fork to clinch some point or other, to make her feel better. 'Of course,' Hugo was saying, 'those Chairs at the new universities are a dollar a dozen, but I don't... it doesn't...' Jamie, though paler than ever, was vigorously nodding his head. Fifteen years ago, as ageing postgraduates, they had collaborated on an article about the Viking cult of the Spread Eagle for the *English Historical Review:* yellowing off-prints of this work occasionally surfaced amidst the debris of the study.

Outside, rain was falling against the plate-glass window in tiny, pointillist swirls, like the ornamentation in a drawing by Aubrey Beardsley. 'Mummy,' Lucy demanded out of the blue. 'Are we going home today?' 'No darling, tomorrow. But you can go in the swimming pool if you like.' The children in her book, she now realised, bore no relation to her own: had she wanted to convey their complex idiosyncrasies into print she could not have done so. Did Hugo and Jamie feel the same about the no less flesh and blood Norsemen who had tugged their victims' ribs out of their chests on spear-points? It was hard to tell. Above her head, the conversation had become general. 'That's right,' Anna was saying, in the languid tones that meant she was seriously cross. 'Building right over the back of the meadow by the side of the college sports ground, I mean. And it's not as if...' Tom, meanwhile, was doodling with a biro on one of the paper napkins: ominous tessellations and triangles, punctuated every so often with a sightless face. By degrees, and after some spirited querying, by Anna, of the bill they debouched into the street. Here the rain had stopped; on the far side a man in a pair of red-checked trousers, a tourist escaped from one of the coach parties, was taking down an umbrella stamped with the legend *Dominus Illuminata Mea.* It was then that 'it', whatever it was – and afterwards Claire was unable to log the precise clash of temperaments that had caused it – happened, that Tom, who had been balancing on the foot-high wall demarcating the margin of a car park, pirouetted there suddenly for a moment and then crashed down into a heap, banging his jaw on the tarmac and bleeding copiously over Anna's white shirt-front as she scooped him up. 'Oh Tom, poor Tom,' Claire said, pulling tissues out of her bag and dabbing at the blood beneath the grave stares of the children. 'I'm sorry,' Hugo said, directing his words to a piece of masonry far above his head. 'I just can't put up with this... With all this...' He made a vague gesture with his hand, that somehow encompassed the rain, the silent, bleeding child and, Claire felt, the rest of them as they stood embarrassedly on the street corner. 'Look,' Hugo said to Anna. 'You'll just have to take him home. I can't...' They watched him plod slowly away in the direction of the University Parks, bandaging his head with a long scarf as he went, not looking back.

Later, as the dusk fell across North Oxford, they returned to the Holiday Inn. The Asian taxi-drivers had disappeared. In their place a brood of dropsical women with suitcases talked melancholically into mobile phones. 'These aren't... they're not... Hugo's best years, you know,' Jamie said by way of explanation, as they eased open the door of the family suite. 'I mean, you should have known him when...' He stopped and began to press his finger-tips tentatively against his forehead. Together they began the ritual search for the packets of aspirin and ibuprofen hoarded against such emergencies. 'Are you OK?' Claire asked. 'I'll be all right,' Jamie said gloomily, 'as long as I can lie perfectly still.' They left him supine on the bed and went down to the swimming pool and drank mugs of hot chocolate in a deserted canteen that looked out onto a yard filled with lines of green refuse bins. *Dominus Illuminata Mea*, Claire thought. Later still, when the children were asleep, she came down to the pool again, empty now in the flaring after-hours light, and swam on unappeasably, in a succession of brisk, purposeful lengths, her mind bent for some reason which she could not fathom on the memory of Hugo's squat, receding figure, the tide of bungalows reaching out to embrace the college sports ground in their bland, domesticating arc.

—2005

Charcoal

As he came back through the French windows he could see the three of them perched on the bench at the end of the tiny lawn. Hemmed in on three sides – the gardens came tightly packed in this part of Putney – they looked oddly detached, unworried by the badly stacked barbecue a few feet away, which was diffusing gusts of pearl-grey smoke, or the juddering music centre beyond the fence.

He stood looking at them irresolutely for a moment – Lucy sat a little to one side, the others were bent towards each other like conspiring sisters – and then straightened up, guiding himself and the tray through the obstacle course of protruding doorstep, scattered paperbacks, a rickety sun-lounger with a frayed canopy. The mild, but sharply accented, voices came drifting into earshot.

'But of course Toby was always a flake… Didn't Emma used to say that was the second most important thing you had to remember about him?'

'What was the first thing?'

'Darling, it's not really a fit subject for the back garden.'

He moved slowly across the patch of uncut, emerald-shaded grass into the shadow thrown by the garden's solitary ash tree. Three months into knowing Lucy, a month into being elevated to the status of Lucy's 'partner' (forty-two seemed a bit old for being described as somebody's boyfriend) his antennae were finely tuned to this kind of conversational shorthand.

He had a feeling that 'flake' meant something different from the usages of his own late twenties . Like 'smart', 'solid' and 'clever', 'flake' was a word that Lucy could coat with layers of an irony he'd not yet been able to penetrate.

There was an upturned flagstone next to the bench, where somebody had left a packet of Silk Cut and a paperback called *Bitchpack Confidential.* He lowered the tray gingerly on to the rough surface and stood up, leaning one arm on the dolls'-house-sized garden shed, shading his eyes against the strong Easter Bank Holiday sun.

Seeing him for the first time, the girls looked up.

'Well done that man,' Serena said.

There was no point in denying that Serena made him uncomfortable. Not only was she younger than the others – twenty-six, maybe, or twenty-seven – but she reminded him of Naomi, his ex-wife. A much younger Naomi, that ghost from his early London days, sunbathing on the roof of the Clerkenwell flat or watching *Live Aid* on TV, dressed only in a pair of tracksuit bottoms, before the Nineties nonsense had gathered them up and defiled the memory of it all.

Curiously enough, he still had Naomi's last letter – two years old now, predating the final ransom demand from the lawyers – in his jacket pocket back upstairs, a disintegrating talisman of past time, never to be surrendered.

He stood there a bit awkwardly, feigning an interest in the grill, until he noticed that Lucy was patting the unoccupied nine inches of bench between her and Charlotte.

Lowering himself warily into it, he caught Lucy's eye. It was the usual glance, one he remembered from the small hours: friendly, complicit, meaning; so far as he could deduce, *Don't worry about my friends*, or *All this is incidental to us*. Like 'smart', 'solid' and 'clever', you could never be quite sure that your interpretation was the correct one, that some important part of the linguistic equation hadn't escaped you.

'Oh no!' Lucy said suddenly. 'Bugger and damnation.'

'What's the matter?'

'Left my sunglasses inside somewhere.'

That was another thing about this tribe of twenty-some-things, he reflected – their habit of framing momentary irritations in the language of cataclysm. Really serious things, on the other hand, featured high up on the roster of evasion and concealment: 'rather an upset' (a written-off car); 'a little problem at home' (somebody's mother's cancer).

'I'll get them,' he announced.

'There's really no need,' Lucy said.

'And the other thing about Toby,' Serena volunteered breathlessly, 'was that you never knew whether to take all that stuff about his parents abusing him as a child seriously or not.'

Back inside the house he made his way stealthily along the cramped corridor that ran from the kitchen to the sitting-room. Here it was unexpectedly cool, and the Sunday papers lay strewn across the sofa. He flipped one or two of the sheets over – there was nothing there except the keys to Lucy's BMW – then began to riffle through the pile of oddments on the mantelpiece.

Long experience had told him that mantelpieces – this was a jumbo-sized version running beneath a Claude-style landscape of rolling woods and hillside bowers – were an infallible guide to personality. This one harboured several invitations couched in varying degrees of formality: *Brigadier and Mrs Tom Slater-Sutherland request the pleasure... The partners of Ernst & Young... Come to Emma's 30th...* a picture of Lucy in a swimsuit standing uncomfortably close to a square-jawed man with wavy hair and a superior smile whose identity hadn't yet been divulged to him, and a letter from Lucy's mother folded inside a cutting from *Gloucestershire Homes and Gardens.*

In the end he found the sunglasses on the hall table, half hidden under a pile of letters addressed to Mr Gavin Henderson, Lucy's ex-boyfriend, 'downsized' from the premises – this was Lucy's joke – some months before.

There was something unsettling him, he realised as he padded back along the corridor with the sunglasses curled up in his outstretched hand like an outsize beetle, something that had nothing to do with Gavin Henderson, the supercilious hunk on the beach, or the tiredness produced by yesterday afternoon's case work and having to drive the children back to Reading in the evening, something from long ago that was trying to force its way out.

There were more photographs clustered on the pin-board above the telephone table: Lucy in a ballgown, at some away-day organised by her law firm, with her parents – gnarled but county-ish – outside an ivy-clad Cotswold pub. Her skin, he noticed, was extraordinary – unworn, the colour of mother-of-pearl, as if the whole of her upper body had just been released from some protective shell. Slightly to his surprise he found himself quivering with what was, presumably, however middle-aged and worn-down, desire. Lucy was twenty-nine.

In the kitchen Serena stood briskly unpacking chicken drumsticks from a series of Tupperware boxes. Feeling a sudden need to ingratiate himself with her, he reached into the fridge and started pulling out the lettuces and tomatoes he'd bought last night on the way back from Reading.

'Actually,' Serena said, 'I was going to leave them for a bit later on. If you don't mind.' She was a tall, bony girl with piles of corn-coloured hair who worked in a shop that sold Art Deco furniture. Still trying to fasten on to the memory that had risen above the sight of Gavin Henderson's unclaimed post, he collected up the salad and put it back. Outside, he could see Lucy crouched over the grill with a handful of firelighters, shooing the smoke away with her fingers.

'You know,' Serena said with the same brisk efficiency, 'I think it's perfectly brilliant of Lu to have discovered you. Where did she say the two of you got together?'

For some reason, the thought of having to explain the complex chain of coincidence that had brought the legal firm where he worked and the legal firm where Lucy worked into temporary proximity was too exhausting to be borne. 'It was a work thing,' he temporised.

'Oh, a work thing,' said Serena. 'I know all about work things. Now, *these* need to go out *there*.'

He went back across the grass, jokily bearing the plate of chicken drumsticks on one hand like a waiter. Nudged into being by the picture above the mantelpiece, the memory

was taking concrete shape now: dense banks of trees moving
into the distance, crumbling stone, Naomi running in front
of him on the path. He'd tried to get together with Naomi
again a year ago, but it hadn't worked. It was too late now.
Lucy was still bending over the grill, plump knees drawn up
under her chin.

'I can't get the wretched thing to work. It just gushes
smoke.'

'You've overloaded it. Look. Take some of the charcoal
out and let the air circulate.'

'Bugger and damnation! It's gone all over my shorts.'

Scooping up some half-charred firelighters with a garden
trowel, then repositioning the metal grill on its plinths, as
Lucy dabbed at her knees with a paper napkin, he considered
this unexpected vista of past time: Naomi's face, the trees
running on into the horizon. From nowhere, half a dozen
other images from that day in Ireland fell smartly into place:
driving along the wide, open highway from Dublin to Cork;
granite poking up through the green hills. Something else
struck him and he said: 'I meant to tell you. I talked to Paul
and he said we can have the cottage next weekend.'

'It sounds nice.'

There were other people arriving now, and he watched
them lounging forward over the lawn. The men, who had
names like Danny and Ben, he assumed were younger versions
of himself: junior managers in accountancy firms, apprentice
lawyers. They hunkered down on the grass, cradling glasses
of wine in their hands, or went into the kitchen and twitted
Serena about the food.

The chicken flared beneath his hand. He thought about next weekend and what sort of a time he could expect. Lucy's sunglasses lay on the bench beside him. Charlotte looked up from a conversation she was having with one of the apprentice lawyers. 'Oh poor you,' she said. 'You seem to be doing all the work.'

It was two o'clock now. He wondered what the children were doing, and whether he oughtn't to be spending Easter with them rather than in a suburban garden with a horde of people he hardly knew. Without warning, the name of the place where they'd had the picnic and Naomi had danced ahead of him down the forest path stole into his head: Loftholdingswood. It had always struck him as a beautiful name. Twelve years later it seemed more beautiful still.

Lucy had disappeared back inside the house. As he badly wanted a drink and there was none to hand he supposed he had better follow her. Serena passed him on the patio. 'Sterling work,' she said. Did it sound patronising? He couldn't tell. The kitchen was full of Dannys and Bens. Professionally, he had evolved a technique for dealing with men a decade and more younger than himself: man-to-man, while encouraging an awareness of responsibilities on both sides. The Dannys and Bens were affable. They said things like, 'Absolutely right', and, 'Where's bloody Nigel got to, then?'

Back in the garden Lucy and Serena were deep in conversation again on the bench. He saw that the grill had nearly extinguished itself: smoke rose vertically into the dead air. Grinning at the memory of the woods, Naomi's rapt, unfallen smile, he moved towards it, hearing the voices drift back on the air.

'A bit... long in the tooth.'

'*Honestly*, Lu.'

'Of course, he's very attentive. But it takes simply ages to do anything, where it *matters*. I mean... You just have to lie there and think of England.'

'God, all this smoke.'

He bent over the grill and studiously, almost reverently, began to rake the charcoal back and forth, waiting confidently for the pale streaks of heat – like memory, he thought – to take root and flicker. In a bit he would go home and phone the children. It was their voices, he realised suddenly, that he wanted to hear.

—2002

To
Brooklyn
Bridge

He came by so early that the sun had climbed only half-way to its accustomed place above the slatted roofs of Mr O'Hagan's building on the far side of the street, and her mother, her voice detached and ghost-ridden behind the bedroom door, said nervously, 'Who's that, Ruthie, calling at this hour?' and she paused in the brushing of her hair before the big oval mirror that hung in the sitting room and replied, 'Now mother, you know that it's only Huey,' punctuating the words with strokes of the brush, and then looked curiously into the mirror as the last echoes of the three smart raps at the door faded into nothing, as if she had never seen herself before and wondered who in all of Chicago the pale-faced girl in the floral print dress could be. There was warm, molten light pouring in through the street window, making the room look dusty and confined, and as she went to the door her eye fell on such things as old newspapers, a handbill for the state agricultural fair, a card that a girl who shared her workbench at Lonigan's had given her, all of them irradiated by the light and somehow magical and aglow.

When she opened the door he was standing a little way back on the landing at what her mother would have called 'a respectful distance', and she smiled and said: 'You must have gotten up really early to be here by now.' 'That's right,' he said gravely – he was always grave when he saw her – 'I guess it was six o'clock or so. It's pretty interesting around then, you know,' he went on hurriedly, as if this getting up early were a mark of light-mindedness, 'I mean, there are fellows in suits waiting for the streetcars and you wonder where it is they're going.' 'I suppose there are all kinds of things people have to do,' she said. 'That's right,' he said, and then, tired of all this abstract talk, 'How are you, Ruthie?' 'I'm very well,' she said. 'I almost didn't get the day off, but then Mr Lonigan remembered he owed me for that Saturday I had to go in back in the fall so I guess everything worked out.' 'I guess it did,' he said. He was wearing the blue-and-white striped jacket and the flat straw boater that made him look like just a little like one of the soda-jerks at the fountain in Pennsylvania Square, and he had a brown paper parcel in his left hand that contained his bathing things. Back in the apartment she could hear her mother moving round the kitchen, the noise of a kettle being filled, the thump of a cat being evicted from a chair. Somewhere in the distance a door slammed shut.

'Why don't you come in and have some breakfast?' she said. 'You must be hungry if you got up at six.' 'Don't let me put you to any trouble,' he said. He had taken off his straw boater and was twirling the brim anxiously around his fore-finger, and his Adam's Apple stuck out of his throat like a tomahawk. He lived way over on the East Side in one of the new projects and she had met him at a dance given by the Young Women's League of St Francis. 'Oh, it's no trouble,' she said, smiling suddenly at the promise of the day before them, the thought of Wabash Avenue and its summer crowds, girls and their dates flocking into the streetcars, and he caught something of the excitement in her voice and came almost blithely through the apartment door to stand in the vestibule shaking imaginary specks of dirt off his shoes and look benevolently at the clutch of umbrellas and her father's ulster and the piled-up boots that her brothers had left there, as if this profusion of objects accorded with every idea he had ever possessed of domestic comfort. She could not take him into the parlour, for it was full of dressmakers' samples, laid out anyhow over the sofa and the chairs, and so she led him into the kitchen, which was full of steam and heat and the smell of baking soda, where her mother looked up from the stove and said, 'Is that you Huey? Gracious but it's early.' Mrs Christie did not like Huey. She had tried to, but she could not manage it. She said there were too many Catholics and the APA had the right idea. And Huey, knowing this, was frightened of her.

It was going to be a hot day, for the Fourth of July flags, not yet taken down from the drug store that ran along the front of Mr O'Hagan's building, drooped listlessly towards the street, and the air coming from off the lake through the open window was warm and full of grit. 'Huey, how are your folks?' her mother asked as she handed out the cups of coffee, and, looking round the tiny kitchen, with its faded poster advertising the Chicago Grand Exposition, the grocery list pinned up on the cupboard door, the cat gone to ground in its basket, she saw that it was exactly the same as it had always been and that not even the introduction of Huey could lend it novelty. Huey was nervous with his coffee. He blew on its surface to cool it, spilled some of it onto his saucer and then poured the liquid that had spilled back into his cup, and all the while Mrs Christie watched and judged him. Later, when he was gone, she would say: 'He's a nice young fellow, I dare say, but he can't manage himself.' 'They're all pretty well, I guess,' he said, when he had dealt with the spilled coffee. 'Although my mother's not so good.' Huey's mother was never very well. She had a goitre in her throat and an abscess on her leg that needed to be dressed twice a week at the doctor's surgery. This was another thing Mrs Christie had against Huey: bad health was a moral failing. The coffee was nearly all drunk up now, and in the silence that followed she could hear the creak of his shoes as he rocked back and forth on his feet. She wondered if her mother had finished with Huey yet, but Mrs Christie had her trump card still to play. She waited until Huey had set down his coffee cup in such a way as to send another little rivulet of liquid over the saucer's edge and onto the kitchen table and said in what was meant to be a conversational tone: 'Of course, Ruthie got her letter just the other day.' 'Why, that's great,' Huey said, with the same air of pious absorption he brought to a baseball game on the radio or a cinema newsreel. 'I'm certainly pleased to hear that.' She stood there by the kitchen table as the cat looked up enquiringly from its refuge, her mother canny and belligerent, Huey pained and conciliatory, and wished that all this could stop. 'That's right,' Mrs Christie said proudly. 'Some girls, they just got standard letters. But Ruthie, she had the principal write to her personally. Now I call that well-mannered.' 'Oh mother,' she protested, 'there's no reason to make such a thing about Mrs O'Riordan writing to me. It's only because there was a doubt about me going.' 'Nonsense,' Mrs Christie said triumphantly. 'She wrote because you scored so high in the test and she wanted to tell you so. Isn't that right, don't you think, Huey?' 'Yes, I'm sure that's so,' Huey said anxiously, knowing that some game was being played with him but not yet able to see what it was.

Having watched Huey spill his tea, satisfied herself that his mother was still ill and wrought upon him the triumph of the letter, the fight went out of Mrs Christie. She had carried her point, established her moral superiority: the young people could make of this what they chose. 'Ruthie,' she said, deciding to leave abstract questions of etiquette for practical necessity, 'if you are going out in this heat, I absolutely insist that you wear a hat. Think what Mrs O'Riordan would say if you turned up on the first day looking like a field hand.' Mrs Christie had been raised in rural Illinois: 'field hand' was about the worst insult she could think of. And so she went back to her bedroom and fetched the straw bonnet she had bought for her holiday the previous year and wove a piece of ribbon around it, which the *Ladies' Home Journal* had said was a sure-fire remedy against dullness. When she came back to the kitchen her mother was gone and there was only Huey twirling his boater in his hand and staring seriously at the picture of Herbert Hoover, gleaned from the *Sun-Tribune*, that had been stuck to the larder door. 'Your mother's in the parlour,' he said. In the early days he had called her 'your ma'. This had got back to Mrs Christie and been appropriately ridiculed. 'She said not to say goodbye. Maybe we ought to go.' 'Yes, maybe we should,' she said. She was annoyed about the spilled coffee and the letter. The ribbon had come adrift from the back of her hat and she wound it carefully up again, round and round her finger, and then pushed the knot into a little crevice in the brim, all the while following him down the staircase and out onto the sidewalk.

It was still not much more than 8am, but already the street was showing signs of life. The Italian family who owned the drug store were out taking down the shutters, and there were old men with elaborately oiled hair in summer jackets labouring past with newspapers under their arms. 'Those eye-ties sure get everywhere,' Huey said, as if to suggest that such work, though not for him personally, would do very well for inferior races, and, wanting to conciliate him, to recompense him for the quarter-hour spent with her mother, she said: 'Yes, they surely do.' The streetcar stop was a block away and they went on rapidly, past the advertisement hoardings and big, high buildings out of whose upper windows men in shirt-sleeves leaned at forty-five degree angles with their elbows on the sills, with the heat growing stronger at every step, and she thought of the other girls at Lonigan's, heads down over the green baize work-table, with Mary Daley, to whose care these commissions usually fell, collecting up two cent pieces to buy a pitcher of lemonade, and realised that in four weeks time, or maybe only three, she would not be there any more and Mr Lonigan would have to get by without her. The awareness of this impending revolution in her life scared her, and she said: 'How are you getting on with your job, Huey? Is it going any better?' And Huey, who worked for a man who had invented a patented sanitary drinking cup, frowned and said seriously: 'I should say it is. That Mr Banahan is a live-wire. Do you know what he did the other day? He took a crate of cups down to the Loop, stood on a trestle table and shouted at people about how great they were. Sold the whole crate, too. Yes, he's a real live-wire, and I'm proud to be working for him even if it is only a commission job.' The position with Mr Banahan was Huey's third commission job. Previously he had sold brushes and a curious kind of vacuum cleaner that did not need plugging into an electrical circuit.

When they reached the streetcar stop there was already a crowd of people waiting: a priest in a cassock with a grocery sack, labouring men with bags of tools slung over their shoulders, a tall fellow with an unnaturally pale face in a suit of overalls whom the other passengers studiously avoided. 'Jeez,' Huey said, wrinkling his nose and divining the cause of this ostracism, 'will you smell that guy? It's no wonder nobody wants to stand next to him.' 'I expect he works at the meat-packing plant,' she said, having caught the scent of fertiliser. 'I don't suppose it's anything he can help.' Nevertheless, it was a very powerful smell and she found herself edging further down the line. The streetcar came clattering up with the sun gleaming off its iron fender and the light blazing into its deep green windows and carried them away, and she sat looking out at the familiar streets and the dusty store-fronts and the street corners, where fat cops stood sunning themselves before the pink-and-white striped awnings and there were vendors out with milk-cans and packets of candy, thinking that the college at Wheaton would be very different to this, and wondering how she would find it, and what the other girls would be like. Huey, with his mouth half open, sat watching the traffic, and counting the Cadillacs, which was the automobile he favoured, or would have favoured, had the privilege of driving one ever been allowed him. It was hotter than ever, and the people in the street – the groups of girls talking to each other, and the negro women weighed down under grocery sacks with bored children toiling in their wake – seemed far away, as if the windows of the streetcar were made not of glass but of some dense, viscous membrane cutting her off from the teeming world around her and turning her in on herself. Back home her mother would be brewing herself a pot of green tea, reading the newspaper and going in every so often to ask her father if he intended to get out of bed. Mr Christie worked on the night-shift at the telephone exchange and was not always amenable to these enquiries.

'Jeez,' Huey said again, 'but I could use a soda.' Beneath his striped jacket there was already sweat welling up in the arm-pits of his shirt. The shirt was too small for him and there was a red crease showing where it dug into his neck. If he took his shirt off when they got to the beach it would look as if he had tried to hang himself. 'Did you ask Mr Banahan about the secretary's job?' she asked, and Huey frowned again, not liking – for all the pride he took in working for Mr Banahan – to be reminded of these things on a day given over to pleasure. 'Sure I did,' he said. 'You don't think I'm the type of guy to let a chance like that slip, do you? You bet I asked him. And he was nice as pie. Told me what a fine young man I was and how he appreciated my efforts, but that everything was pretty tough right now and they needed a qualified man. So I guess it'll go to some cake eater who's done his time at night school, yes sir, and not to yours truly.' It was a long speech for Huey and the tomahawk of his Adam's Apple went working up and down again as he said it. She had only once been to the apartment on the East Side, where his mother lay in bed all afternoon eating candy out of a paper bag and his father sat listening to the boxing matches on the radio. Mostly they sat in cafés together, or prowled around the early evening streets.

The number of people in the streetcar had thinned out by now. The priest had gone, and the man in the blue overalls who smelled of fertiliser. There was a black puddle on the floor that looked like spilled ink. The advertisements that ran along the car at the level of her head were for carbolic soap and pocket zip-fasteners and a magazine called *Modern Pictorial* which promised to 'lift the lid on Hollywood'. The remaining passengers were all destined for the lakeside, too. They had bundled up towels under their arms, and some of them carried little wicker baskets and flasks. She wished she had had a wicker basket to bring, but Mrs Christie had said they were unnecessarily expensive. There were six or seven couples in the same degree of proximity as Huey and herself, and she examined them surreptitiously, one by one, and decided that three of the men were better-looking than Huey and three worse, and one of them – a bald man with almost no eyebrows and variegated teeth – so ugly that it was a wonder he was allowed out. The streetcar was slowing down in sight of its final stop, and she found herself lapsing into her favourite day-dream, which was of being married to a grey-haired but still youthful man in a dark suit, who called her 'Ruth' and 'my dear' instead of 'Ruthie' and established her in a neat plasterboard house with a white picket fence somewhere in the Sixties, where the coloured maid sometimes brought her drinks on a silver tray and Mrs Christie occasionally, but only occasionally, came to supper on Sunday evenings, when there would, additionally, be 'company'. She knew that it was foolish to chase these phantoms, but she could not help it. They had sustained her through her time at Lonigan's and she suspected they would see her through her time at the college at Wheaton as well.

There was a pain in her right hand where she had been clutching the arm-rest of her seat, and she massaged it with the fingers of her left. The streetcar had slowed practically to a halt and the people around her were stirring, rather as if they had been woken from sleep. A girl a yard or so away from her with a pair of zealously plucked eyebrows that made her look like Betty Boop said: 'Gee, Stan, will you look at the way the sun shines off the water?' and the boy she was with grinned and said: 'Fritzy, you're a poet and you just don't know it.' The girl's dress was made of cheap, plain cotton, and she wondered how she had come by Stan, who had a shock of dark, unruly hair and was wearing a college football sweater. They stepped cautiously from the streetcar at a point where the sand had come nearly up to the sidewalk and there was a man with a peaked visor and arm-bands on his shirt selling ice-cream out of a portable refrigerator. In the distance there were white birds criss-crossing the blue sky and beyond that long ships apparently motionless on the horizon, so slow-moving that they were almost inert, like pieces of balsa wood laid out on an azure blanket. 'This is the life,' Huey said vaguely. He was a tall boy, taller than the man in the college sweater, but his weight was not adequate for his height and made him look spindly. 'You must be careful,' she said, 'not to sit in the sun with that pale skin of yours.' There had been an occasion when Huey had come back lobster-coloured.

'Oh, I'll be careful,' he said. He had the remote, far-away look that he sometimes wore on these excursions to public places. 'It's awfully hot,' she said, aware of the sun on her bare arms, the warm sand spilling over the tops of her shoes, the draw-string of her bag digging into her shoulder. 'That's right,' he said. Something was concerning him beyond the sheen of the water, the long, low ships and the crowds at the beach, and he said, not curiously but as if courtesy impelled him to ask: 'How long is it till you stop off working for Mr Lonigan?' She had an answer to this which had already been doled out to several other enquirers. 'On next Friday fortnight,' she said. 'I can't stay a moment longer. I don't know why but I just can't. I guess the other girls will buy me a cake. They usually do. When Susie Montgomery left to get married they bought her ever such a nice one. But she was there five years and I've only been there two.' She thought about Lonigan's, with its crackling fan sending the stale air around the green baize table, and the odds and ends of cloth lying around in heaps, and the trimming scissors as big as shears, and realised that the only thing that made it tolerable was the fact that she was leaving it. 'Two years,' Huey said, who had never been in a job longer than six months. The sunlight was shining off the buttons of his jacket and he stepped gingerly over the sand, fearful of bumping into people or putting his feet into the picnic baskets.

They found a spot near the shoreline, where some young kids were ducking each other in the shallows while a lifeguard looked benevolently on and a mustachioed old man in a one-piece bathing costume swam backwards and forwards against the tide, labouring like a grampus, and established themselves on the sand, and she clasped her hands over her knees and looked out into the far corners of the lake, beyond the line of ships, where the water was greyer and less tractable. Huey took off his shoes and socks and sat with his feet stretched out in front of him. They were enormous feet – size twelve, at least – and her mother had once said that if Mrs Niedermeyer ran short of a clothes line then all she had to do was to hang a string from one of his big toes to the other. Sometimes he picked up pebbles and threw them into the water, and at other times he squeezed the parcel that contained his bathing clothes into a pillow and lay flat on his back staring up at the sky. To right and left the crowds of people extended as far as the eye could see: couples running in and out of the water; families grouped around their rugs and baskets; men in straw hats with their pants furled to knee level walking up and down. 'Don't you want to bathe?' she asked. Huey threw a little stone, so weakly that it barely made the water-line. 'I don't know,' he said. 'I guess I don't feel like it. Maybe I will later.' The young kids had stopped ducking each other and were staring hopefully out over the water, as if they expected a frogman to emerge from the depths, but the old man in the one-piece bathing costume was still labouring strenuously up and down, ever more pious and determined, as if only a sense of responsibility, some weighty obligation to wife, children and dependants, was stopping him from heading north to Canada, thrashing his way along the rivers that flowed out of the Great Lakes and swimming up the Yukon like a salmon. She had seen all this before, a hundred times at least, but now she realised that the prospect of going to Wheaton was making her see it anew, but to Huey it was just the beach crowd and the splashing children and the doughty old men. There were some words in her head that had not been there when she sat on the streetcar or asked Huey whether he intended to bathe, and suddenly, without her being conscious of the effort, they assembled themselves into something coherent and she said:

> *How many dawns, chill from his rippling rest*
> *The seagull's wings shall dip and pivot him,*
> *Shedding white rings of tumult, building high*
> *Over the chained bay waters Liberty…*

'What's that?' Huey asked. He knew the words were not hers and suspected them.

'It's a poem we learned at literature class,' she said. She was proud of the literature class, which took place in a young women's institute and was addressed by a middle-aged lady who had studied at Bryn Mawr. A few more lines came into her head and she went on:

Then, with inviolate curve, forsake our eyes
As apparitional as sails that cross
Some page of figures to be filed away;
– Till elevators drop us from our day.

The old man in the one-piece bathing costume was not swimming quite so fast. She thought that if she looked at the lines of ships – they were container ships, bringing goods in to the port – then, all but imperceptibly, she would see them move. The sun was burning hotter now and she wished she had brought a parasol.

'What does it mean?' she asked.

Huey distrusted the literature class. It was not how girls were supposed to spend their time. But he was fair-minded in his attitudes, had gone with her to see movies he had known he would not enjoy and been proved right, and once to a classical concert. That had been very terrible, but he had gone. Now he said:

'I don't know. I suppose it means what it means.'

Shedding white rings of tumult, building high/Over the chained bay waters Liberty, she repeated. It was intriguing to say it, as if all the people on the beach had vanished and there were only the two of them attending to the grave matter of a poem and what it meant. *Shedding white rings of tumult*, she said again.

'I guess it's a seagull flying over the water,' Huey said, not quite comfortable with all this and fearing its implications. It was hard not to associate it with the new life stretching out before her, of studious girls and unthought-of destinies. He was not insensible to beauty and sometimes cut out poems that had appeared in newspapers and presented them to her.

'I guess I can come and see you at Wheaton,' he said. 'At weekends, I mean.'

'I shall want you to,' she said. She had no idea of what it would be like there, or what she expected from it, or from anyone. The sun had risen full into the sky now, and the people beneath it were wilting in its heat. She rose to her feet, carefully brushing the grit out of the folds of her skirt, and walked a little way over the sand to the water's edge. It was at times like these that she wanted to fling a bottle into the deeps with a message in it saying who she was and where she lived, so that some other girl, in Canada maybe, or perhaps even in England, would come across it on some lonely shore and know that she had written it, and there would be an article in a newspaper remarking on the miracle of this transition, this flight of a sealed-up bottle from one world to another, but she knew that she would never be able to do this, that it was too quixotic, and offended against her sense of responsibility, which of all things was the one she prized herself on the most. When she came back from the water's edge Huey was sprawled back onto his outstretched arms with one of his feet balanced on top of another to create an extraordinary ziggurat of flesh on which a flag could quite easily have been flown. She had meant to stop talking about the poem, but somehow it was in her head again and she declaimed:

> *I think of cinemas, panoramic sleights*
> *With multitudes bent toward some flashing scene*

Never disclosed, but hastened to again,
Foretold to other eyes on the same screen

Huey did not respond. He was lost in the majesty of his feet. Still out in the deeper water, fifteen yards away, the old man in the one-piece bathing costume laboured back and forth. The crowd around them was thickening fast. There were shop-girls on their lunch-hours come to sunbathe, old ladies setting out the contents of their picnic baskets, strange, shock-haired children whom no one seemed to be in charge of roaming at the water's edge.

Foretold to other eyes, she said. The middle-aged lady from Bryn Mawr had suggested that poetry bred up in you emotions that you would not otherwise have felt. There was a poem by Emily Dickinson that had once aroused her to a state of exaltation, and she had recited it to her mother. Mrs Christie, who preferred the verses printed in the *Sun-Tribune* about the banks of the Wabash, had said it was very nice and gone on measuring out cupfuls of flour. Poetry was all very well, but it went only so far. Huey seemed to have lost faith in the spectacle of his feet. He set them down, side by side, too self-consciously to let the gesture pass, and said with great determination:

'I shan't be staying with Mr Dreiser forever, you know.'

At the college in Wheaton there was a special black gown which the girls wore for Sunday church services. She knew that her first act when she arrived there would be to purchase one of these gowns.

'No, Huey,' she said patiently. 'I don't suppose you will.' She could never quite decide what amount of faith she ought to place in Huey's ambitions, whether simple loyalty on her path would enable him to win through and secure his dreams – whatever they were – or whether more complex factors were at work. Mrs Christie had said that Huey was a nice boy, but plain unlucky, that his employers would always die on him, or go bankrupt, or flee to Indiana with their creditors on their tails.

'What a fellow needs,' Huey said, with what was meant to be steely determination but in some way fell a yard or two short of this, 'is a chance.'

There was a sound of heavy footsteps coursing rapidly over the sand. Ten yards away two people – a lifeguard in a yellow shirt and a smaller man in a neatly tailored suit – were running towards the water's edge. The smaller man looked as if this sharp exercise was inimical to him, a betrayal of his dignity but nevertheless a part of the compact he had forged with the world. There were other people, she saw, clustered around the old man in the one-piece bathing suit, who had fallen to his knees and was supporting himself on his outstretched hands, like a child readying itself for a wheelbarrow race.

'Overdid it, I guess,' Huey said knowledgeably. He was still thinking about his chance. The group of people broke apart – they did this with great courtesy and a little awe – to admit the lifeguard and his companion. A cop appeared from nowhere, planting his booted feet delicately on the sand, and began to shoo the onlookers away. The lifeguard dragged the old man in the one-piece bathing suit out of the shallows and the second man clasped one hand over his chest and felt with the other for a pulse in his wrist.

'He doesn't look too good,' Huey said dispassionately as they laid the old man down on the sand. He was quite motionless now, his face a kind of grey-green colour, like ancient rock from the botanical garden, and did not respond as they worked on him.

'All a fellow needs…' Huey began again, and then stopped, aware even in his own distress about Mr Dreiser and the teacher-training college at Wheaton that this was not a time to be talking about chances, his own or anyone else's. The lifeguard and the doctor – if that was what the second man was – continued with their work, their backs bent in unison. On one side of them the old man's legs stuck out stiffly in the sand. Once a child's ball came rolling towards them, but the child's mother came anxiously running to scoop it up in her hands and bear it away. She realised, to her shame, that she was annoyed by the old man's falling down like this, for it had given the day a context from which nothing she or Huey could say or do would ever rescue it, that she was, however indirectly, caught up in something from which there was no escape. A hundred yards or so away she could see a pair of men bringing up a stretcher, stumbling in the sand and sometimes almost falling over their feet in their determination to bring it home to port. She had once attended a first-aid course that involved practising mouth-to-mouth resuscitation on a splay-limbed dummy, but somehow she did not care to bring this expertise forward in the service of the old man.

Huey stood irresolutely at her side, sometimes taking a sideways glance at the old man but mostly staring at the sand that lay in the shadows created by his two thin legs. The cop was saying 'Nothing to see here people. Just move along, will ya? Nothing to see' to anyone who came within earshot. Slowly the life of the beach began to resume its original pattern – the children playing with their toys, the old ladies freshening themselves with fans made of rolled-up newspapers – only that the old man still lay at the water's edge with the doctor pushing every so often at his rib-cage. Once a pause in the movement of the doctor's hands exposed the old man's face, and she saw that it was as grey as lead. She found herself thinking about the black gown she would wear on Sundays at Wheaton and the bright sunshine streaming through the vaulted windows of the Episcopalian chapel. In this way great stretches of time seemed to pass, but when she looked at her watch she found that only a few moments had gone by since the old man had been dragged out of Lake Michigan. But the bloom had gone off the day: there was no doubt about it. Huey looked at his monstrous feet again, as if they might have the answer to the problems with which he was clearly beset.

'Well,' he said. 'I guess we can't stay here all day.'

'No,' she said, although she knew there was no reason why they should not stay if they chose, 'I don't suppose we can.'

They were putting the old man on the stretcher now. She could not tell if he was alive or dead. For a moment his long, meaty, sunburned arm fell away from his body and hung there dangling until the lifeguard jammed it back into place. At the apartment Mrs Christie would have finished lunch and her father would be shuffling blearily around the kitchen drinking black coffee from a china mug. The sunlight was not so clear as it had been and the shop-girls and the milliners' apprentices who had come here to eat their sandwiches were going back to work. The scent of petrol hung in the air and she thought again, with pleasure, of the college at Wheaton, which lay in sight of the cornfields and the buzzard-haunted prairie grass.

'We could walk back and look into some of the stores,' he said.

'Yes, we could do that, I suppose.'

Back on the sidewalk at the margin of the beach, where grey sand mixed with the cigarette butts and the dropped newspapers, he tried to take her hand, but she did not want her hand to be held. An automobile had leaked oil in the middle of the street, which spread out across the tarmac in rainbow-tinted streaks. There were still gulls tacking back and forth in the thermals, and she remembered the shedding white rings of tumult. And so they set off again into the city's heart, with the streetcars gliding alongside them like triremes, and Mr Dreiser, the college at Wheaton, the black stuff gown and the grey-haired man who would call her 'Ruth' and 'My dear' and the company who would call, who would certainly call, on Sunday nights hanging above their heads like the sailing white birds.

—2013

Wrote
for Luck

'I t's still quite light outside,' Clive said soberly. 'We could go and have coffee in the garden.'

It was half-past nine in the drawing room of the Allardyces' house in Wimbledon. Above her head Lucy could hear the rhythmical progress of someone – child? au pair? grandmother? – padding from bedroom to bedroom. Mark, either taking this as a subtly coded instruction, or simply wanting to be polite, got up and began stacking the bowls that had contained the kiwi-fruit mousse into a neat, unwavering pile.

'What's happening, in a sense,' Clive went on seriously, gathering up the fragments of a conversation that Lucy assumed had perished a course and a half back, 'in a very real sense, is that for the first time you've got a squeeze at both ends. In the centre as well. In the old days you had simple rules: cut costs, diversify, watch the margins. This time the top of the market's getting smaller and the bottom's splintering. Mega-mergers and fragmentation. Global saturation and niche players. And there's no middle market any more. You either get larger or you get smaller or you die.'

'You could draw a political parallel,' Mark went on with, if anything, even greater seriousness. 'Huge alliances all banding together – Europe, South-East Asia, wherever – but at the same time every half-dead barony out of the Holy

Roman Empire wants its own set of postage stamps and a seat at the UN.'

Not consciously bored with these exchanges, but feeling over-familiar with an argument that surfaced regularly at dinner parties of this kind, Lucy stood up and went to look out of the French windows. Above, the sky was blue-black, touched up at the corners with crimson streaks. Beyond, the garden stretched out for twenty or thirty yards into the gloaming. You could not afford a garden like that in south-west London on less than half a million a year, Lucy knew.

'I got a call the other day,' Clive went zestfully on, 'from an insurance broker, financial intermediary, who wanted to know how e-commerce was going to affect his business. And I had to tell him – God, Lucy, I felt like a doctor with a cancer patient – the chances were that in eighteen months he wouldn't have a business.'

Henrietta, Clive's wife, yawned and put her hand guiltily over her mouth. Inspecting the three of them from her vantage point by the window as the blue light fell over her hands, Lucy was reminded of a tableau she had once seen in a medieval book of hours: the nobleman dispensing wisdom to his dutiful squire, the nobleman's wife fatly asleep in the corner. Looking at Clive as he sat back in his chair, the candlesticks on either side of his plate framing him in a way that was faintly sinister – he looked like a portrait in a ghost story that might be about to leap down out of its frame – she wondered what it was about him that Mark, inherently sceptical when presented with a newspaper article or a balance of payments forecast, found to admire. Expertise? Panache?

Intellect? Having had several opportunities to observe Clive at close quarters, she didn't think he was particularly bright or particularly astute. Perhaps, in the end, it was a kind of instinct for self-preservation, knowing how to play a game whose rules were being made up as you went along and where your opponent was liable to collapse out of sheer terror.

'I thought those seminars,' Mark said, accepting his coffee from Henrietta without looking up, 'the ones where Gavin and Fred talked about the practical impact of that Far Eastern stuff, were really useful.' Looking at him as he said this in what had started off as a spirit of moderate scepticism – he was, what was it, thirty seven now and the butter-coloured hair was speckling at the edges – Lucy realised that she had a lot to be grateful to Mark for. Even that joint mortgage on the new house they'd talked about – pretty pointless when you thought about it, Lucy decided, seeing that Mark earned five times what she made at the BBC – came dusted with a thin coating of principle.

Somewhere in the back of the house a mobile phone began to ring. Stepping out through the French windows – the end of the garden was bound up in shadow now – Lucy discovered a second salient difference between Wimbledon and Putney: silence. For some reason the inhabitants of SW19 didn't spend their summer evenings blasting out hip-hop or skirmishing in the shrubbery. Decorum was all. Thinking about Clive and Henrietta (who 'kept her hand in' at the PR department at Laura Ashley, she had explained, with a bit more mock- enthusiasm than was called for) made her wonder about the whole question of admiring people, how

81

often you picked on what turned out to be the wrong quality or detected an element that turned out to be something else, something that said more about what you were looking for than about the thing found. She remembered at twenty one conceiving an intense, unfeigned respect for her college tutor, a middle-aged spinster who had written a famous book on the Gawain poet, coming back to visit her three years later and finding a dowdy little woman living in a tiny house in north Oxford and being neurotic about whether you'd wiped your feet.

They were sitting on a kind of patio now, lit by firefly lights suspended from an overhead trellis, next to an occasional table on which someone had left a fruit-juice carton and a copy of *Captain Corelli's Mandolin*. Catching sight of her face in the window, she was disagreeably surprised by its paleness, the odd point that her chin made against the inky surround. 'What I don't understand,' she heard herself saying, rather startled to hear the sound of her voice breaking out above Henrietta's murmurs about more coffee, and the faint commotion of a child at an upstairs window, 'is why all this really has to happen. I mean, I know you can't do anything about global pressures – at least I know everyone says you can't – but if two banks, say, are making a profit and employing 20,000 people each, then what's the point of welding them together so you can cut the workforce back to 30,000? I just don't see it.'

As soon as the words came out of her mouth she knew – and she had meant this to happen – that it was the wrong thing to say. The mobile phone began to ring again. Henrietta went off in search of it. Clive picked up a teaspoon and banged it against the side of the coffee percolator.

'It's interesting you should say that, Lucy, because... let me put it another way, the people who were saying those things five years ago – and they were saying them, weren't they Mark? Do you remember that proposal we did for Vickers where..? Anyway, the people who were saying that five years ago are mostly... I mean, there are insurance companies out in the Rim running their operations with a couple of hundred tele-execs... You can't just not take economies of scale when they're offered to you.'

Henrietta was standing in the gap between the French windows making what looked like quite complicated sema-phore signals.

'It's Nick wanting a word.'

'Oh God,' Clive said, not altogether failing to disguise his pleasure at being rung at ten o'clock at night by the firm's senior partner. 'Well, if he wants it he'd better have it, hadn't he?' He strode off, a big man poised expertly on oddly tiny feet, and they watched the back of his striped pink shirt dis-appear into the house.

'Sorry,' Lucy said. 'Not a particularly brilliant thing to say.'

'Gracious,' Mark said tolerantly. 'You mustn't mind about that. Clive's a bit preoccupied by the proposal.'

'The pipeline in Azerbaijan one?'

Clive and Mark had arrived at twenty to nine by taxi, grey with fatigue, clutching ring-bound files and what looked like the print-out from an old-fashioned computer but was actually the outpourings of a Russian telex machine.

'Clive won't be a moment.' Henrietta came labouring back onto the patio, flapping vaguely at a midge cloud that hung in the doorway. Even on the low-key occasions, a category which surely included this entertainment of your husband's understrapper and your husband's understrapper's girlfriend, being Clive's wife must be rather a strain, Lucy deduced. Her eye fell again on the paperback of *Captain Corelli's Mandolin*.

'It's wonderful isn't it?' Henrietta said before she could be asked. 'I don't know how many times I've read it. And the film. That was wonderful too, wasn't it? Quite made you want to go and stay there. Wherever it was set, I mean.'

'It didn't make me want to go and stay there,' Lucy said diplomatically, 'but I think I know what you mean.'

'And it makes you wonder, doesn't it?' Henrietta went on fiercely. Her white, plumpish face was oddly animated, Lucy thought, like one of those TV game show contestants suddenly enriched beyond expectation. 'I mean, why it is that writers come to write things.'

'Beckett wrote for luck.'

'For what?'

'I read it in some book of interviews. The *Paris Review* or somewhere. He said that whenever he sat down consciously to write, he was doing it for luck.'

Once again Lucy knew, instinctively, that she had said the wrong thing. Henrietta looked perplexed. More than perplexed, Lucy divined.

'Do you know,' she said – and years later Lucy would recall the look of injured innocence on her face – 'I think you must be making fun of me. He couldn't possibly have done that. There must have been another reason.'

'I suppose it was all to do with him being Irish.'

'You *are* making fun of me,' said Henrietta, not crossly, Lucy thought – which might just have been warranted by the circumstances – but with an almost plaintive dolefulness. 'I never heard anything so silly.'

They watched her pad off again through the French windows. In the kitchen they could see Clive stalking back and forth, bellowing excitedly into the mobile.

'Looks as though you got the job,' Lucy said. 'Do you know, what Clive gets paid a year is probably the entire budget of the series I'm working on at the moment. I figured it out.'

'Honestly Lu, that's not much of a comparison.'

'All the same,' Lucy said, smiling brightly at Henrietta as she wheeled back into view bearing a tray of champagne flutes, 'I just felt like making it.'

Later, quite a bit later, they rolled home in a cab down Putney Hill, through tiny streets sunk in darkness. Curiously, this was the time Lucy liked best about her life with Mark: that companionable ten minutes or so of padding around the silent house, checking the answerphone and the fax, setting out briefcases for the dawn. The morning's post and the stack of estate agents' brochures lay where she had left them on the kitchen table. Looking at Mark as he lurked at the foot of the bed, his game and still slightly frantic face looming happily through the shadows, Lucy wondered – something she'd never got to the bottom of in the three years of their relationship – if this serenity, this pleased matter-of-factness was genuine, whether it didn't just denote some part of him held permanently in reserve.

'I didn't make it up,' she said. 'Beckett did say he wrote for luck.'

'I'm sure he did.' She could see him blinking thoughtfully at the pile of management magazines on the bedside table. 'I think it was just a bit much for Henrietta.'

Something about the evening's small talk came back to her. 'This pipeline job. Will you have to go out there?'

'I shouldn't wonder. Clive will probably want me to project-manage it. Do you mind?'

'Why should I mind?'

'It will probably mean waiting a bit on the house.'

Lucy had seen this coming. 'How long?'

'Well, two or three months. The spring, maybe. Prices may even have fallen a bit by then.' He picked up one of the magazines. 'You can do most things from Azerbaijan these days, but I don't think buying a house is one of them.'

Lucy was surprised by the sense of loss that this brought, surreptitiously, into view. The Allardyces' lawn; the child's white face at the window; the thought that you shouldn't be expected to put up with this degree of obtuseness from someone you loved; all these thoughts briefly but inconclusively contended in her head.

There was silence for a moment. Lucy fell asleep almost immediately, woke up for a second or two to see Mark brooding over a book called *Managing the Blur: Corporate Life in the Connected Economy*. She went back to sleep thinking of the little woman in the house in north Oxford whose book on the Gawain poet, she reflected, might have sold five hundred copies, Henrietta's placid face under the light, a feeling that could have been contempt, or envy, or some quite different emotion lost now amid the coffee cups and the darkling south London lawn.

—2001

Teeny-weeny
Little World

At some point in the remote past somebody had dropped a bottle of ink on the lip of the rush-mat carpeting. Over the years the stain had faded from light-blue to cobalt, finally to an indeterminate shade of grey. He would have missed it had it not been there. The secretary, who had shuffled the sheets of paper on her desk three times and pretended to read them twice, said, exaggeratedly, 'The Headmaster will see you now, Mr Crowther,' like someone impersonating a secretary in a *Carry On* film, and he stood up and put the copy of the Old Boys' newsletter, with its picture of the rugby team touring New Zealand, back on the circular table. Like the headmaster, the secretary was new, and had been heard to say that the fifty-yard walk to the noticeboards was an imposition. The boys, shrewd in these matters, had already nicknamed her 'Ma Baboon'.

The path to the headmaster's study lay across a tiled passage, sealed off at one end by locked double doors. Here there was a view out of the window into the Cathedral Close and several portraits of evil-looking old men in clerical robes. He wondered how many times he had taken this journey. Two hundred? Three? Routine made you unobservant, less vigilant of the nets that might be thrown out to pinion you. He pressed on into the study, past the gas-fire that sometimes worked if you kicked it in the right place and towards the immense oblong desk where the new headmaster sat making desultory remarks into a telephone. 'A child-focused paradigm,' Crowther heard him correct his caller, 'irrespective of the core competencies.'

The new headmaster was short and stout and had the vestiges of a West Midlands accent. However, he had stopped saying 'righty ho', which showed a conciliating spirit. When he saw Crowther he waved excitedly, put down the telephone and said, in a single, unpunctuated stream of words: 'Very good of you to come and see me won't you take a chair great deal to discuss.'

Crowther took his chair, which was the one that slumped alarmingly to the left, and found himself marking the changes that had been effected since his last visit in the summer. The engraving of the Wensum at Pull's Ferry was still there and the view of the city from the high ground, but the drawing of the chapel had made way for a photo of what looked the debauched aftermath of the Chelsea Arts Club ball, but turned out to have been taken at the last meeting of the Headmasters' Conference.

'Very good of you,' the new headmaster said again. Crowther resolved to concentrate more thoroughly, so that if anything was said with specific application to himself he should not look foolish. 'Hear very good things about your extra studies classes GCSE boys,' the new headmaster said unexpectedly, but with just enough of a glint in his eye to let Crowther know what was going on.

'Oh yes,' Crowther heard himself saying. He would admit nothing. Answer only direct questions. That was the way. 'I mean...' the new headmaster said. Another thing about the new headmaster was his habit of not finishing sentences, of allowing these streams of words to dry up on the river-bed leaving only inference to re-hydrate them.

'What exactly..?' he said again, and Crowther found himself explaining, in rather incriminating detail, about the classes, which encouraged, and occasionally compelled, rather wooden boys to read and discuss moderately abstruse contemporary poems. The new headmaster was already nodding his head. 'Poetry...' he said vaguely.

Crowther wondered what he meant by this. That he approved of it? Feared its corrosive influence? Outside it had begun to rain and there was a fine drizzle blowing over the Nelson statue and the spindly trees. It turned out that the new headmaster was advocating caution, if not variety. 'A topical discussion, perhaps.'

Crowther knew all about topical discussions. 'The wider context,' the new headmaster ventured. It turned out that a parent, one Crowther particularly disliked, had written to disparage poetry and press for basic economic theory. 'A very interesting suggestion,' he heard himself saying. It was always a mistake to listen to parents.

The rain was coming down quite hard now, and a few boys, briefcases lofted above their heads, scuttled furtively between the chapel and the music centre. 'Valuing the work put in,' he heard the new headmaster say. There was something else going on here, he thought, an undercurrent of trouble he could have done without, a way in which, however subtly and respectfully, the values on which he had fashioned his existence were being called into question. Someone in the common room the other day had said that the new headmaster, known to be in favour of co-education and new universities, was also keen on early retirement. 'Look forward to hearing…' the new headmaster finished up. What did he look forward to? Crowther didn't know.

The secretary laboured grimly into the room, looking more than ever like some text-book illustration of Darwinian theory, and he went back along the passage and out onto the tarmac of the playground, where the morning's detritus included three oranges, an empty aspirin packet and a dog-eared copy of *Les Fleurs du Mal*.

It was not, in the end, the new headmaster's fault, he thought to himself, driving home down a road along which lorries ferrying rubble from the site of the new shopping mall alternately surged and concertina'd. The new shopping mall, he knew, would merely displace the city's commercial heart: a dozen new premises opening up half-a-mile from a dozen others ceasing to trade. But it was what people wanted. Teeny-weeny little world, he thought. A painter – was it Edward Burra? – had said that about a war-time Rye threatened by bombs: the same principle applied. No, the new headmaster was as much a victim as himself, not an *ubermensch*, but a minion sent to do that titan's bidding. But this understanding did not make him any more sympathetic to the new headmaster: if anything, it made him crosser.

Parking the car in its square of luxuriantly unweeded gravel, he found himself wondering exactly what the values were that he feared were being called into question. No one, after all, was asking him to suspend his powers of judgment. Or were they? He knew that it was nonsense to pretend that basic economic theory was more valuable to a teenager than the poems of Geoffrey Hill. Or was it? He had a nasty feeling that he was being got at for believing in things whose superiority he could not absolutely prove. Doubtless there were people somewhere who thought a West Midlands accent demonstrated authenticity, roots, a vindicated purpose. Well they were wrong.

The house, whose silence he had looked forward to, was full of small, unsettling intrusions. In the kitchen he found his wife's cousin Finula and her fast friend Cecily – quartered on the premises this past week – having one of their terrible conversations. He was used to his wife's cousin Finula and even, up to a point, to her friend Cecily – engrossed, amnesiac creatures in their late fifties – but dealing with them required tact. 'Mead is a very excellent drink,' he heard his wife's cousin Finula saying. Rather than preposterously free associating, Cecily gave one of her trademarked laughs – a full-throated sea-lion's bark that had once, in a country lane, caused serious disturbance to a flock of sheep. Head down over the stove as he made his coffee, he attended to the conversational ebb and flow, which resembled a series of inexpertly flung javelins each landing a field's length from its intended target.

Once Finula had engaged him in a literary conversation. Did he think *Atonement* was a nice book? It depended on what you meant by a nice book, he shot slyly back. After all, hadn't George Orwell once said, apropos of Dali, that great art could still want burning by the public hangman? But you could not have this kind of conversation with Finula. Just as he had no vocabulary with which to discuss her profession, which was some kind of local government work, so she had no vocabulary to discuss books. Remembering this he deduced that in some way Finula and the new headmaster were confederate: each lacked the ability to discriminate.

Beyond the window the Norfolk fields descended into autumnal twilight. His wife came smiling into the room, and Finula and Cecily ceased to exist. 'The Mannerings want to extend their garage,' she said – the Mannerings lived at the bottom of the garden – 'and put up a conservatory. Do we mind?'

'Of course we mind,' he said. The new headmaster; Cecily and Finula; the Mannerings. They were all the same, he thought, agents of the *ubermensch*, wreckers and despoilers.

Obscurely, after months of one-man guerrilla warfare, he found he had an ally. Most of the school staff were young, keen and sporty. Mr Deloitte, the art master, was old, cynical and treated the badminton set to an occasional negligent supervision. 'You'll get nowhere with the new man,' he explained. 'He's one of the change for change's sake brigade. There'll be girls in here in a couple of years, I daresay. The boarding house is beyond saving. But you can have a lot of fun bamboozling him. They never understand irony, of course. And whatever you do, don't refuse that offer of staff rep. on the governing body.'

'They won't want me,' Crowther said, thinking of the letter that had lain on his desk since the end of last term.

'They've no choice, have they?' Deloitte said. 'Senior man, aren't you? Do you know, the wretched character' – he meant the new headmaster – 'actually gave some parent my home number. Had some fishwife ring me up to ask if Johnny would pass his GSCE.'

Slowly, sedately, without noticeable excitement, the autumn passed. A cement mixer and tessellations of scaffolding appeared in the Mannerings' garden. Finula and Cecily departed for Chichester. Several books, a ceramics kit and three copies of *Readers' Digest* followed them in a brown paper parcel. Still the letter from the governing body lay on his desk. Details of an early retirement package of quite startling munificence were posted on the common room notice board. All these things seemed to him to be connected: they demanded a decision from him that he did not want to make. Finally there came a day when he sat once again in the headmaster's study in the defective arm-chair.

Outside the rain lashed the Cathedral Close: the secretary sat at her desk making coy, simian grunts. The new headmaster was, if anything, even fatter and had taken to saying 'righty ho' again.

'Question of exploring synergies school already possesses,' he said at one point.

Did that mean the extra studies class? Crowther couldn't tell. But he had done his homework, honed his capacity for pastiche.

'Actually,' he said, 'I see it as a part of our wider programme for individual empowerment.'

The new headmaster blinked in a way that suggested he knew he was being mocked, but could not quite see how the trick was being done.

Crowther found his gaze roaming around the rear wall, which showed further signs of tampering. The engraving of Pull's Ferry was still there, but the view of the city from the high ground had gone: in its place hung a picture of the new headmaster talking to a man who looked quite like Lord Attenborough from a distance but was actually someone else.

Clarity broke suddenly upon the confusions of the past weeks. 'Really sorry to hear decision wonder if reconsider,' he heard the headmaster say in one of his heroic vocal truncations.

'Actually headmaster…' he heard himself reply in rather startled correction. As he did this he found the vanished painting rising before his gaze: the squat heap of the castle, vertiginous spire, the rolling plains beyond.

Even teeny-weeny little worlds needed their protectors, he thought, their worms gnawing at the intruder's vitals, their sanctifying blight. 'Delighted naturally unexpected,' he heard the new headmaster say.

The look on his face was oddly like Finula's in the conversation about *Atonement* – less reproachful than puzzled, realising that a judgment had been made, not knowing why it had come about. Suddenly Crowther felt better, better than he had felt in a long time, lofty, magisterial, eager to appease. The leather arm- rest jabbed agonisingly beneath his ribs.

'You know, headmaster,' he said, in what he hoped was a friendly tone, 'now that I'm joining the governing body I really ought to see to it that you get some new chairs.'

—2007

Blow-ins

There were people who came to East Creake simply to paint its sky, but they did not come in November. After Michaelmas the light turned iron-grey and the breaking dawn smeared up the cloud behind it so that the effect was not one of Turner-esque tints and hues but like a very pale egg-yolk dragged out over a plate. Just at this moment the light was falling slantwise over the double row of attractively priced paperbacks that Caroline had set out in the window-boxes. Nearer at hand, little aggregations of hardback novels – some of them as recently published as six months ago – rose above the white display table bought for a song from the East Creake furniture mart. Ten feet away there was a terrific jangling noise – like some satanic turnkey wrenching open the gates of Hell – and Nick, with the diffidence that he brought to almost every human activity, came shambling into the shop.

'I went down to the Fisherman's Pantry to try and get some herrings,' he said, 'but they seem to close up at two these days.'

'The tea shop's already shut for the winter.'

Come Bonfire Night the East Creake emporia began to keep odd hours. Even the librarian of the Sailor's Reading Room, where old salts in oil-skins dozed over the *North Norfolk Mercury*, grew capricious. The Book Bag's decision to stay open for eight hours a day six days a week was regarded as a dangerous innovation.

'Sold anything?' Nick asked in a tone that suggested it was a matter of startling wonder that any shopkeeper ever sold anything to anyone.

'Mrs Carmody bought that copy of Edward Heath's *Music: A Joy for Life*. She thought it might do for the choir book group.'

Outside the high street was deserted except for an old man – so old that he had probably been present at the unveiling of the Art Deco war memorial – propping his bike up against the flint wall of the Dog and Partridge.

'I *knew* that would go in the end,' Nick said sagely. The £2.95 at which Mr Heath's leavings had been priced would make their fortunes: anyone could see. The twitch in his upper lip as he pronounced these words suggested to Caroline that he had something disagreeable to tell her. 'Actually,' he said, 'I've got to go to town again tomorrow.'

'Well, bring back some more copies of *Music: A Joy for Life*,' she said, not quite humorously. 'We'll have a sale.'

Later they had supper in the tiny back-room behind the shop. As the Fisherman's Pantry had not come up with any herrings, this was limited to ham and eggs on toast. Outside, rushing winds plucked at the shutters and the flimsy guttering. From time to time the light-bulb danced on its wire.

'Why have you got to go to London?' she wondered.

'Tom said he wanted to go through that script again. He thought Barbara might have trouble with some of the jokes.' Nick wrote plays that were broadcast on the radio and very occasionally performed in obscure provincial theatres. 'Oh, and Mrs Trent-Browne threatened to put her head round the door. Her choice of words, not mine.'

'What does Mrs Trent-Browne want?'

'There's some kind of village festival planned for the summer. And she said wanted to see how we were getting on.'

Practically everyone she knew wanted to know how they were getting on, Caroline thought. Her mother wanted to know. Her half-a-dozen best friends wanted to know. If it came to that, Caroline quite wanted to know herself. They were prudent and, or so they thought, unexcitable people, but they had bought the lease of the Book Bag on a whim, wandered down the high street one summer forenoon, seen the TO LET sign in its dusty window and, euphoric in the July sunshine, clinched the decision over a crab salad in the Enniskillen Tea Rooms. Trade, brisk enough around the August Bank Holiday, was not quite what it could have been now the tourists had gone. 'I don't quite see the *point* of a bookshop,' a woman in a headscarf who had stopped once outside the half-open door had been heard to say, 'what with the travelling library and everything.'

'If I have time,' Nick said, who would not have time, 'I'll call in at that wholesaler and see about some new stock.' His mind was far away, in third acts and jokes that actresses could understand.

'You do that,' Caroline told him.

The next day she shut up the shop after lunch, traversed a row or two of pebble-dash cottages, slipped by the ice-cream parlour and the amusement arcade, each now shuttered up and moribund, and went for a walk along the beach. There were a few fishermen down at the north end, lines drawn tight against the surge of the ocean, and rain coming in on the wind, and the town's solitary teenage boy throwing stones against a tin. On the way back she made a detour to the nature reserve and left a handful of leaflets (*If books are your bag, then try the Book Bag*) in the café. A previous drop had been discovered two days later in a waste-paper bin. Not everyone in East Creake's resident population approved of blow-ins, a category in which Nick, at least, was shocked to find that he was supposed to reside. 'I spent the first eighteen years of my life in Fakenham,' he had protested, 'and my parents live in Burnham Market. What more do they want?' When she got back to the high street there was a foxy-looking middle-aged-to-elderly lady in an Inverness cape standing on the pavement outside the Book Bag with one hand clasped to the door-knob. Caroline did not like that hand. It suggested collusion, infiltration, colonising intent.

'My *dear*, so *there* you are. How *nice* to be able to shut up shop whenever you feel like it,' Mrs Trent-Browne said in her usual blizzard of phantom italics.

'Yes it is, isn't it?' Caroline conceded. In the life of East Creake, Mrs Trent-Browne was a mysterious figure, known to enjoy exercising the considerable power she possessed in a capricious manner. She was rumoured to own half the high street, and at her instigation a Women's Institute lecture on 'The Exotic East' had been replaced by a demonstration of flower-arranging techniques.

'I've been *very* remiss in not coming to see you,' said Mrs Trent-Browne, following Caroline briskly into the shop. 'Especially now that I hear you're doing so splendidly.'

There was no getting rid of Mrs Trent-Browne. She poked around in the bargain bin and bought a P.D. James for 75p, admired the display of cookery books while suggesting that they could be moved slightly to the left, and clucked her tongue over a biography of the Dalai Lama, all the while discussing her plans for next summer's festival. This was to be on an extensive scale, do wonders for trade, involve the covering of the high street in a deluge of tricoloured bunting and the commandeering of the village hall for a display of horse brasses. By the time she left Caroline had agreed to host an evening in the shop at which one of Mrs Trent-Browne's friends would read from a volume of self-published poems entitled *Wood Sorrel.*

In her absence the shop seemed diminished, turned in on itself, barren and inert. The bargain bin, in particular, appeared to be such a desperate coign of literary vantage that Caroline decided to re-utilise the space for Psychology and Self-help. There were no further customers. Nick came back late, by taxi from Sheringham station, which suggested that the script meeting had gone well, and she told him about Mrs Trent-Browne and the festival.

'I heard something about that,' he said. He had bought himself a new scarf, which sat uncomfortably on his thin shoulders like a Lutheran priest's ruff. 'Apparently they're looking for premises for an office.'

'How did you get on?' she enquired. As the Fisherman's Pantry was still keeping odd hours they were eating gnocchi bought at ruinous expense from the up-market delicatessen three doors down.

'Not so bad at all,' Nick said. He could be complacent at times. 'I'll probably have to go back next week and stay a night or two.'

A storm blew up in the small hours and took half-a-dozen slates off the roof. Without explanation, Nick's night or two turned into a week and a half. Over the next few days Caroline heard a great deal about the festival. There was an article about it in the weekly paper, a picture of Mrs Trent-Browne statuesque upon the village green and many a rumour about the site of the festival office. There was also a letter from Mr Warburton, the solicitor who had arranged the purchase of the Book Bag's lease.

'I thought you said he was such a nice old man,' Caroline complained, once she had negotiated the complex series of upward revisions on which the renewal of the lease seemed to depend.

Nick's ear for local gossip was better tuned. 'I think I heard somewhere that he's Mrs Trent-Browne's brother-in-law.'

In retrospect Caroline could never quite tell when she became aware that the place where Mrs Trent-Browne burned to establish her festival office was the Book Bag. No one informed her directly: it must have happened by osmosis. Meanwhile it came as a shock to discover that she was at the heart of a guerrilla war which she could not remember having started. One lunch-time she came back to the shop to find that someone had plundered handfuls of the attractively priced paperbacks from their ledge and flung them all over the pavement. But if Mrs Trent-Browne had her partisans, then, as a practised opponent of local planning applications, she also had her detractors. Two days later there came a hand-written but necessarily anonymous note that read: *tell the old bitch to go to hell.*

November was wearing on. The nature reserve closed up for the winter, and the stone curlews and the oyster-catchers in the reed beds browsed on unregarded. Elderly gentlemen in flat tweed caps could be seen walking to the village hall to play whist. Matters came to a head one Thursday afternoon, when the light had begun to fade and a series of flashes and detonations over the eastern sky made it look as if an alien invasion was in train, and Mrs Trent-Browne descended once more upon the shop. It had been a bad day, bringing a bill from the wholesaler and a letter – an actual letter, such was the gravity of the news it contained – from Nick.

'My dear,' Mrs Trent-Browne began. She was unusually flustered, no doubt fearful that the aliens had her in their sights, were about to carry her off into the clouds above Brancaster Staithe. 'I've come to make you an offer.'

Caroline stared at her stonily. Nick, the ever diffident, apparently wanted time to 'think things over'. Having blown into her life, he seemed all too ready to blow out again.

'An *offer*,' Mrs Trent-Browne went on, as if repetition and emphasis would somehow seal the business. 'Let me have your lease for my HQ and you can move into the Bodega absolutely rent-free. Mr Warburton can fix everything up in a jiffy.'

The Bodega was a failed art gallery on the high street's outermost margin that smelled of rotting fish. For some reason it was Nick's scarf that rose in her mind, a scarf that now suggested abandonment, urban sophistication, greener grass. 'No I won't,' she yelled at Mrs Trent-Browne. 'You're a nasty, interfering old woman, and I wouldn't let you have the lease if you were the last person alive.' 'My *dear*,' Mrs Trent-Browne plaintively, but it was too late, far too late. The nearest thing to hand was the biography of the Dalai Lama, and she absolutely picked it up and threw it at Mrs Trent-Browne's anguished and departing head. Afterwards she strode in triumph along the stony beach, past the slumbering fishermen and their lines, and the endless worm-casts, on and on into the beckoning blue-grey horizon, where there was no Mrs Trent-Browne, no Nick, no mocking metropolitan neck-wear, only herself, her books and silence.

—2013

Brownsville Junction

His uncle, old Spencer Van Hart, had come back from Vietnam with a Master Sergeant's stripes and two fingers missing from his left hand, and though the army gratuities didn't pay so well in those days he walked away with a pension and a two thousand dollar disability benefit. For a time he wondered about investing in a plantation or buying some real estate out near Lafayette, but it turned out that tobacco growing was in slump and Spencer didn't like the look of the Nashville lawyers who ran the real estate business, so he put the money into the café at Brownsville Junction. The previous owner had only been gone six months, but Spencer fixed on doing the thing properly. He put ads in the *Cook County Sentinel*, fitted in chromium-plated soda dispensers along the rickety bar, and because he was a Louisiana boy who had gone through most of South East Asia with a stars and bars insignia in his forage cap there was a neon sign that read 'The Rebel Den'.

Even at the grand opening, when they had a couple of country bands playing on the open forecourt and Spencer's buddies from the National Guard sat on the porch drinking root beer, the omens didn't look good. Brownsville Junction lay on the western side of Choctaw Ridge at the point where the pine forest ended and the railway lines came snaking in from Nashville and the Gulf: a dusty main street and a strew of log cabins that led on to the trainsheds and the abandoned freight yards. For a while the old timers who remembered Spencer's father came out at the weekends to stand in the asphalt car park trading reminiscences, but then in the mid-Seventies they cut back the railway service and Spencer found himself serving to a handful of local farmers and the odd hobo who'd fetched up in Choctaw forest. But he stuck it out. 'Taking a dip in Van Hart's trashcan,' Barrett the journalist used to say when the talk turned to some conspicuously underfunded local amenity. Towards the end he turned into one of those ramrod-straight middle-aged men who live off their pride and no-one would dare offer a hand to, so it wasn't until he was off in hospital at Johnson City and there was a FOR SALE sign up over the door of The Rebel Den that people started saying that it was a shame and what did Spencer's folks reckon they were doing anyway?

There was no close family. Spencer's parents were both dead and his brother had left home years back, but a couple of nephews showed up at the funeral. They were fruit farmers away in Kentucky, people said, and neither of them had set eyes on Spencer since the day he left for the training camp at Fort Sumner. There was a third nephew called Ron who worked as a film stunt man out West and whose name sometimes appeared in the credits of Al Pacino films, but he hadn't been seen in Cook County for twenty years and it was left to the fruit farmers to smoke dollar cigars on the church porch and talk to Spencer's lawyer about legacy duty and probate.

I was working down near Choctaw that week on a photography project for the State Forestry Board, so I didn't get to see Spencer's funeral, but Barrett stopped over one night on his way from a track-club meet at La Grange to fill me in. 'You didn't miss anything my man. Two Kentucky strawsuckers in K-Mart sneakers and pantsuits, looking like they couldn't wait to collect. Reverend Daniels hadn't hardly finished his oration before they were off to get the will read. You never saw anything like it.'

I said it seemed like a lot of trouble to take over a run-down café that nobody wanted to buy. Barrett smiled that lazy, ornate smile that made him look like a Southern gentleman in an ante-bellum TV drama. 'You got it my man. Leastways, those two bullet-heads walked out of the attorney's office with a couple of unpaid electricity bills and Spencer's collection of army cap badges. Last thing I heard, they were still arguing about who was paying for the train fare.'

As it happened, Spencer's nephews turned up two or three times in the next month or so. They ate prawn platter lunches with the real estate salesmen at Brackus's bar and diner or had themselves driven out to the Junction where they stood inspecting the plywood shutters that had been put up after old Spencer got taken to hospital. 'Kind of desperate,' people said. They put ads three weeks running in the *Cook County Sentinel* real estate page offering the café at the same price Spencer had paid for it in 1972, but there weren't any takers. Summer stretched on into September. The brothers went back to the farm twenty miles outside of Lexington, the grass curled up under The Rebel Den's boarded-up windows and Joe Brackus cracked his old joke about the Kentucky dirt farmer who tried to reach his dog to write but then stopped when he found out the dog was smarter than he was.

It was a wet fall that year. The rain blew in early from the Gulf and covered the back roads with a four-inch coating of mud, and the river burst its banks over by Degville Gap. Working down in the pine woods, taking shots of the felled timber or following the environmental department guy around to snap pollution damage, I got used to sheltering behind the big trees waiting for the wind to drop, or staring out over the canvas roof of the foresters' pick-up at the angry sky. Then on a particularly bad day, when it had rained for four hours clear and ruined two waterproof Nikon cameras, Barrett turned up in a borrowed convertible, wearing the three-button Fox Brothers suit the paper made him put on when he had to interview a state congressman or an assistant secretary from the DA's office. There was no-one around – the forestry board manager was vacationing in Florida and the two girl assistants had taken the day off – so I figured on showing Barrett round the site, but he wasn't interested.

'Forget it my man. I seen enough trees to last me a lifetime.' He looked shrewd for a moment. 'Lee-Ann around here any place?'

Lee-Ann was the younger of the two girl assistants, a forestry graduate from Tennessee State University and way out of Barrett's league.

'Gone to visit her daddy over in Marin County. You want to leave a message?'

Barrett shrugged. 'Can wait. Hey, guess who turned up in town the other day?'

I suggested the ex-county Treasurer, who'd gone down under an embezzlement charge six months back, but Barrett smirked and pressed the tips of his fingers together in that way he had. 'His parole don't come up for a fortnight. No, Ron Van Hart showed up.'

'Spencer's nephew?'

Barrett flicked me an impenetrable look in which awe and derision grimly contended. 'He's a big star my man. Maybe you don't get to see his name at the top of the credits, but he's up there with Pacino and Hackman. You ever see that inferno scene in *Escape from Alcatraz*, the one where the guy leaps out of the burning building on a pulley rope? Well, take it from me, it sure as hell wasn't Clint Eastwood.'

It was a characteristic of Barrett's that he never explained how he came by his information. I watched as the convertible jerked away towards the low line of trees, their tips blown back and wavering in the wind. After this Ron Van Hart turned up a lot, a burly conspicuous figure in the gathering October gloom. He stood at the bar of Brackus's blowing froth off his moustaches and buying drinks for grey-haired fifty-year-olds who claimed they remembered him from way back. Barrett wrote him up for the *Sentinel*, a lavish photo spread that featured Ron shaking hands with Richard Dreyfuss and doubling as Luke Skywalker on the set of *Star Wars*, and gradually people woke up to the fact that they had a celebrity in their midst. There was a two-year waiting list at the Stonewall, the gentleman's club where the tobacco planters gathered on Saturday nights to play stud poker and drink juleps, but he had dinner there on his second evening and people started saying that Ron Van Hart was all right, not like some of your Hollywood actors that wouldn't give the time of day to the folks they were brought up with. Meanwhile the FOR SALE board stayed up over the shutters of The Rebel Den.

As usual Barrett put his own gloss on the local gossip. 'Of course, my man, wasn't always this way. Let me tell you, twenty years back they nearly ran Ron Van Hart out of the county. Car stealing, mostly. Folks who came into town on a Saturday night used to leave their doors unlocked in those days and Ron, well, he just used to help himself. Not that that would have got him run out of the county, but the guy had a mean streak. Wouldn't think it to look at him maybe, but he busted a girl's head open with a bottle back in '68.'

'Why would he want to do a thing like that?'

It was a simpleton's question, but Barrett only grinned. 'Who knows? Maybe she wouldn't come across. Maybe she made too many jokes about pig-shit. He worked on his daddy's farm, you see, and people used to piss themselves about it. Anyway, Ron laid her out cold. If his daddy hadn't played in a poker school with the DA's brother-in-law he'd have been lucky to keep out of jail.'

Whatever the truth of these allegations, no trace of them remained in Ron's current behaviour. Kind of weird, people reckoned – he had a habit of staring at you and not quite listening to what you said – but pleasant with it. You saw him doing the rounds of the roadside diners and barbers' shops, shaking hands with folks who'd known Spencer. Come late October he disappeared – out West, people said, doing a movie with Dustin Hoffman – but then a fortnight later he was back again and a contractor's firm from Jackson came and took down the shutters from The Rebel Den and started re-laying the split pinewood floor.

November dragged on and the light faded away into mid-afternoon shadow. The wind started bringing down trees over by Choctaw Ridge and there were a couple of hurricane warnings. The ex-County Treasurer emerged from the state gaol at Dyersburg and announced that he was suing the DA for malversion. I was busy around that time, checking through slides with some field biologists over in the forestry department at Johnson City, so I didn't get to see what was happening out at The Rebel Den, but Barrett kept me informed. Around Thanksgiving his voice came crackling down the portable telephone we used out in the camp at Choctaw. 'Seems as if Ron's opening up the Den again my man. Grand re-opening party, transport laid on and a zydeco band from New Orleans, you name it.'

'Any particular reason?'

'Beats me my man. Just pouring dollars into the swamp is the way I look at it. Said something about respect for his uncle, but you want my opinion he's out to spite those two strawchewers from Lexington...'

There was a pause as the wind whistled over the wire.

'Jesus,' Barrett went on. 'You hear the news? Hurricane Tony's due in from Tampa Bay in seventy-two hours, they reckon. Lee-Ann about these days?'

'Off sick.'

'Ain't none of my business,' said Barrett. 'But if I were you I'd check up on that girl one of these times.'

I was driving out near the Junction the next day, as it turned out, so it wasn't hard to check out Barrett's account. In late autumn the place had a dreary, downcast look. Only a dozen or so of the cabins were occupied now, the smoke drifted up out of the tumbledown chimneys and the main street was a lake of dirty water. At The Rebel Den there were a couple of glaziers putting in a new plate glass window and a roller flattening the bumpy forecourt. Ron stood in the doorway clawing at his chin with quick, uneasy movements, but when he saw me he grinned and beckoned me over.

'Hey. Photographer, ain't you?'

When I nodded he went on: 'Could use you in a couple of nights' time, if'n you're agreeable. Take some pictures of my party.' He pronounced it 'par*tay*'. There's some big stars coming in you know. Maybe you could sell to the newspapers afterwards.'

I smiled, although it struck me that he was just looking through me, that he saw something else way back twenty yards from where I was standing. Then I headed off, only stopping to confirm what I'd suspected as I drove in: that the pink Chevy parked by Van Hart's forecourt was Lee-Ann's.

Lee-Ann turned up at the site two days later with a bruise on her arm that everyone tried to avoid noticing all through the grey, windy morning. That night Hurricane Tony blew in, bringing three larch trees and a power cable down across the foresters' cabin, so I missed the re-opening. Barrett, who struggled in through the gale and had his windscreen busted by a falling branch, reported that it was a weird party. 'No-one *you* ever saw my man, and if Pacino was there it was a grade-A disguise. And Ron, Ron kind of flipped. Just sat there and talked about the guys he knew in Hollywood and how he once got to use Stallone's Jacuzzi.' The wind gusted on through the night. Next morning a squad car called at the Rebel Den, but Ron had already disappeared and the storm had taken the roof right of and laid it over the newly flattened forecourt. Later Barrett filled me on the details, about how Ron hadn't worked in Hollywood for five years and was wanted for a string of unpaid hotel bills and a couple of assault charges.

They found the body a week later, sprawled over the disused railway line. There was an old photo of Gene Hackman in the pants pocket and a putdown letter from an agent dated four years back. 'Taking a dip in Van Hart's trashcan,' Barrett said jauntily when I bumped into him at Brackus's that night. Lee-Ann was sitting at right angles from us so she missed the wink that Barrett gave me. Ron's two brothers had a bulldozer come and clear the site – they had plans to sell it to the county amenities department now – and I stood in the clearing where the line of log cabins met the trees, turning my head against the force of the wind, and thinking that it was nothing you could complain about, that all of this – Spencer, Ron, The Rebel Den and the picture of Gene Hackman – just wasn't something you could expect a fruit farmer from Kentucky to understand.

—1991

The
Disappointed

South of Chelmsford they lost their way in a tangle of B-roads and ended up in a lay-by looking at the map. The sun, dormant until now behind hedgerows, climbed suddenly into the sky and drenched the car's interior in blinding white light, so that, twisting round to look at him from the passenger seat, she could see only a glare of reflected surfaces, orange swirls and dense, aquarium shadows. Outside dragonflies bounced against the windows. 'Where are we?' she asked.

'Not far from Thorpe le Soken,' Douglas said. He was staring at the map with what she realised was a characteristic grimace: the way at any time over the last ten years he had stared at CD players that refused to function, documents that declined to yield up their intent: peevish, momentarily affronted, but innately confident in his own resourcefulness.

They cruised on for a while through fields of green sedge, eight-foot lanes engulfed by cow parsley. The smoke from Douglas's cigarette dribbled out of the wound-down window. In the distance grey stone rose beyond small, densely packed trees. The air was turning fresh.

'Where did Alain get this place anyway?'

'Some friend of his mother's. Just for the summer while he roughs out that treatment.'

There was an edge to the way Douglas said *treatment*. It was his usual way of referring to friends' accomplishments: Toby's *novel;* Greg's *first night;* Nick's *piece about Mrs Thatcher in the Economist.*

'Silly question, I suppose, but what are we going to do when we get there?'

'Watch it, of course.'

'Watch what?'

'Have you been living on Mars for the last fortnight? The football.'

Actually, Alexandra wanted to say as they negotiated a winding gravel drive, hemmed in by lofty rhododendrons, *I might just as well have been.* There was a weekend colour magazine lying in the pile of detritus at her feet with a picture of Gascoigne on the front and she picked it up and looked at it with faint incredulity. Once, not long ago, she had seen him on some lunch-hour chat show and marvelled at, well, what exactly had she marvelled at? The absence of any kind of inner resource? The capitulation of everything – every question, every idea – before an over-whelming, bedrock chirpiness. He was like something out of a cartoon, she decided, every response hypertrophied into burlesque. How could you take him seriously, what he did seriously? Even more, how could you take seriously the people who were impressed or even just interested or amused by him?

Douglas's voice came floating through the ether. She realised guiltily, but not perhaps as guiltily as she might have done, that he'd probably been talking for a minute or more.

'… And so Roger said that what with all the arts supplements expanding and the *Independent* taking on people again, there was a good, no a *strong* chance, that…'

The gravel drive was thinning out now into not much more than a cart track. Great clumps of rhododendrons grew close to its edge, sometimes threatening to obliterate it altogether. Tipping her sunglasses back onto the bridge of her nose, she looked upward and found only inert grey sky, a plane tracking slowly along the horizon's edge.

'This is the real back of beyond,' Douglas said. He was turning faintly irritated now, she realised. 'Where did you put those directions?'

They pressed on through the rhododendrons until finally the track swung left to meet a high flint wall. Slowly and incrementally the house took shape before them.

'It's quite something, isn't it?' Alexandra said. Together they contemplated the troughs and cornices of weathered, salmon-coloured brick. 'Almost *Brideshead*-y.'

'Of course,' Douglas said seriously. 'You have to realise that Alain could never actually afford to live somewhere like this. He can't earn more than twenty thousand a year.'

Which is more or less what you earn, Alexandra acknowledged. Another thought struck her. 'What's this girlfriend of Alain's called?'

'Claudia… No, Candia.'

'What does she do?'

'I don't know. Works for some newspaper.' Douglas looked at his watch. He was definitely cross about something, Alexandra divined, some lingering slight not yet confided to her. 'Come on. If we don't get a move on we're going to miss the opening ceremony.'

Later they had supper in a large white-walled kitchen with red tiles on the floor and a view out over rows of neatly planted apple trees. Cats came in through the open door and sat grooming themselves on the inner steps. Silent at the far end of the long oak table, Alexandra ate *salade niçoise* and French bread and listened to the football talk.

'Did you see that free kick against Egypt? And then Wright's header? *Magic.*'

'And Platt's one against Belgium? Gazza loops the ball over, he's got his back to goal, but he just turns round and *wham*!'

There were times, Alexandra thought, when it was possible to believe that all this knowledgeability, all this *expertise,* was wholly bogus, assumed in the same way one might put on a fashionable piece of clothing. People who knew about football, she suspected – and she knew nothing, she was happy to admit that – would trip the likes of Douglas up, overturn him and leave him sprawling on a mat of exposed limitations. She wondered if this was what was making her irritated – and she was irritated, she could feel annoyance rising in her like mercury – and decided that it was not the sound of Douglas and Alain talking about football, not even the faintly absurd and self-conscious attitudes they struck while they were doing it, but the long-term memory of their lavish but somehow unfocused enthusiasms. She remembered Douglas ten years ago in a college bar or a pub in North Oxford expounding some theory about pop music, something about Pink Floyd and punk rock, and almost bit her lip at the pain it caused her, all that ghosted seriousness about something which in the last resort you had no serious interest, the attitudes of a college tutorial taken out into real life.

Glancing along the table, she stared hard at the two of them in an attempt to work out what that decade had done to them. Made them more self-possessed? Less? Physically they seemed unchanged, or rather more defined. Ten years ago they had been clever middle-class teenagers moving confidently into their twenties. Now they were clever middle-class twenty-nine-year-olds moving a little less confidently into their thirties, spending a July evening in 1990 talking about the genius of Paul Gascoigne.

There was more food arriving now, bowls of fruit and yoghurt, and the movement made her shift her gaze. Candia, Alain's girlfriend, sat opposite and a little to one side: a plain, square girl of about twenty-five with what Alexandra had the nous to realise was a prohibitively expensive designer haircut, a kind of savagely inept Eton crop with tendrils escaping down her cheeks. Sphinx-like until now, Candia suddenly caught at something in the conversation and gave a tiny rap with her fork on the table top.

'That's interesting,' she said. 'You just – forgive me if I didn't get it all – used the word *aesthetic* about this, this *game*. Now, allowing that the people playing it create something that can be described in these terms, how far do you think they're aware of what they're doing?'

'What do you mean?' Douglas asked.

'Well, what's his name? – Gascoigne? – scores a goal, let's say. Now, to you watching from the stand – well, from your armchair maybe – I can see that there's some pattern to it, some, well, *architecture*. But how do you think Gascoigne sees it?'

'Pure sensation,' Douglas said briskly. 'If you really want to know, I see Gascoigne as a kind of human racehorse. The beauty's all in the eye of the person beholding him. I mean, I don't see Gascoigne articulating it in any way, do you?'

'That might be an articulation problem, not a perception problem. Who can tell what Gascoigne thinks when he scores a goal?'

'He's a thick Geordie who left school at five or something. He'd probably be on the dole if he couldn't play football. I don't see the distinction.'

'And yet you admire him? I mean, all this stuff he does, it's an *achievement* of some kind?'

'Of course it is. How couldn't it be?'

'Thanks,' Candia said, 'I just wanted to know.'

Listening to this exchange, which struck her – at least on Candia's part – as angled or even premeditated in a way she could not quite comprehend, Alexandra found herself thinking of a boy in her primary school class called Gary Nichols. Coming from the middle-class end of a socially mixed collection of eight-year-olds, Alexandra had not exactly been forbidden to associate with the likes of Gary Nichols, but a certain amount of circumspection had been unobtrusively enjoined. She remembered … it would be difficult to say what she did remember. Gap teeth, certainly. An unfailing good humour in the face of what even at that age was a large amount of official asperity. Mild exhibitionistic tendencies. Chronically limited social repertoire. Oddly, Alexandra had rather liked him, even to the extent of inviting him to her ninth birthday party (he hadn't turned up), and had regretted his eventual departure to a special school on the other side of the city. But there was no doubt about it. In her eyes, Gascoigne and Gary Nichols had been forged in the same crucible.

Moving into the sitting room she heard Douglas saying, possibly to himself but perhaps to the room at large – as if there were some doubt about his fervour which he wanted to rebuke – 'We've got to win this one. We've just got to.'

'Why? Why have we got to win it?'

'It's Germany again. Like in 1966. 1970. Surely you can see the historical significance of playing Germany. I mean, surely you can remember what you were doing that day in 1966?'

'I burst into tears,' Alain said seriously. 'When Weber equalised. I threw myself on the floor and burst into tears.'

'My dad gave me a pound,' Douglas capped. 'Can you imagine? A whole pound.'

'I was five,' Alexandra volunteered. 'We must have been in Hong Kong. I don't remember anything about it.'

'1966,' said Candia, coming in through the doorway with a tray full of coffee mugs. 'I was in my cradle. What *is* it about this sporting nostalgia?'

Sitting in front of the widescreen TV, drinking coffee and smoking what Alain described as 'some high-grade Moroccan stuff, fresh off the boat', which Alexandra thought was incredibly juvenile but still consented to go along with, she heard that there were various preliminaries – warm-ups, handshakes, loudspeaker introductions – to be got through before the match began. Somehow this annoyed her even more, on one, abstract, level because it lashed a yet more complex and many-layered wrapper around the meagre kernel of these twenty-two hooligans kicking their ball about; more immediately because it gave Alain and Douglas a chance to proceed from the Football Talk and its lesser variant the Football Nostalgia Talk to what Alexandra always thought of as the Absent Friends Talk. Leaning back in her chair, watching the line of haggard, crop-haired men in white shirts being presented to a fat person in a blazer, she listened dreamily to the familiar fragments of rumour and disparagement.

'... Got fifteen thousand from Chatto & Windus, but Peter says he doesn't think he'll ever finish it.'

'Peter said that? If it was Peter he wouldn't even start it.'

'... When I last saw him he said the *Statesman* had stopped running his strip because they thought it was too depressing.'

'Oh it wasn't for that. Karl's never liked him since he used to go out with Julia at Cambridge ...'

'Gracious,' said Candia. 'What a lot of people you seem to know.'

Fortunately this turned out to be an overture to Alexandra, and they had a companionable little gossip themselves about two or three mutual acquaintances dredged out of the world of print journalism and the TV fringes. Here Candia, whom direct questioning revealed as a researcher on *Newsnight*, proved so frighteningly knowledgeable that Alexandra felt rather non-plussed, like a veteran coach offering a work-out to some promising club athlete only to find herself unceremoniously steamrollered into the track. Lounging back in her chair again, as the figures crossed and recrossed on the fizzing screen, she felt suddenly chastened by the picture of herself that this conversation had thrown up, a kind of sadness in which, she realised, Douglas, Alain and the consciousness of past time each played their part. If, as occasionally happened, anyone asked Alexandra what she had been like at nineteen, she invariably smiled and offered only that 'I was very naive', something that Douglas – who had been the chief beneficiary of that naivety – always affected to find funny. In fact, Alexandra secretly thought she rather liked the nineteen-year-old she imagined herself to have been: innocuous, kind-hearted, docile. It pained her to think that she might be turning into one of those bright, brittle thirty-year-olds she had once regarded with such awe.

And contempt, of course. Something had happened onscreen, some player had keeled over or something, and Douglas was softly murmuring 'Bastard, bastard' under his breath. Alexandra couldn't tell whether he wanted this to be taken seriously, or whether it was part of the web of male complicity he and Alain were spinning over the evening.

'Butcher,' said Alain, with immense gravity, 'is amazing.'

'Totally amazing.'

'To take all that punishment and then just ... get up.'

'Did you see him that time on the touchline after they'd carried him off? Before he had the stitches?'

They were a bit like an alternative comedy routine, Alexandra thought – not exactly funny, but encouraging the audience to despise their lack of self-awareness. For a moment, as the white phantoms surged back and forth over the green turf, she thought hard, very hard and seriously, about why she liked Douglas and decided – rather forlornly, for she had hoped that there might be other things that would leap out and surprise her – that it was to do with this lack of self-awareness. Somehow a Douglas who knew about his shortcomings and discussed them in the avid, guiltless way that people did on American talk shows would have been intolerable. In some ways, she decided, it was his ignorance of what he was that gave him charm.

It was nearly half-time. Alain and Candia were having a whispered conversation at the far end of the sofa. Talking to Alain, Alexandra saw, Candia's face grew animated in a way she had not previously noticed. Not certain whether she wanted more coffee or whether the proximity of other people was becoming irksome, she wandered slowly into the kitchen and sat down on one of the tall stools by the table. Here it was cooler and the light glinted off the surfaces to produce a sub-aqueous effect. Outside the first faint traces of dusk were falling over the garden and the fruit trees were gathered up in shadow. In the distance the sun burned off the hedgerows, and she stared out of the kitchen door into this curious, limpid world of shade and silence, motionless except for the birds noisily displacing each other from a rectangular table on the lawn. There was a disturbance behind her and Douglas came into the room carrying a beer glass.

'There's drink in the fridge if you want it.'

'No thanks.'

'They're doing really well, you know. I mean, they could score if they go on like this.'

'That's good then.'

Atmospheric subtleties had a habit of passing Douglas by. She had a memory of climbing with him up Siguraya Rock in Sri Lanka. Emerging onto the flat table of the summit, Alexandra had gasped at the tides of jungle – and at that height they seemed like a vast, undulating ocean – that spread out across the horizon. Douglas, arriving a few minutes later, the sweat coursing in rivulets over his forehead, had simply stared blankly around him: non-committal, faintly bewildered. Now, three years later in Essex, he rummaged in the fridge for a can of beer, straightened up and stood uncertainly looking at her.

'We could come and live somewhere like this,' he said. 'If you wanted to.'

'I thought you said you had to be in London for your work. I thought editors preferred sending the bikes to Highgate.'

'I don't know. We've been there eight years.'

'Jesus,' Alexandra said. 'Six months after we get a mortgage on a sodding flat, and you're talking about moving out of London.'

'I could write that book about Maclaren-Ross.'

'Yes,' she said, not unkindly. 'You could write that book about Maclaren-Ross. And I suppose when he hears about it the old bastard in Sussex who's sitting on the papers will give them to you out of sheer generosity.'

Douglas shrugged. He was, Alexandra knew, quite impervious to this kind of reasoning. Arguments in the flat at Highgate – which she suspected even now that they couldn't really afford – generally consisted of Alexandra shouting and

Douglas shrugging, opening a can of beer, staring at her in a belligerent, slightly puzzled manner, rather, she thought, in the way he had examined the Sri Lankan jungle.

He looked at his watch. 'Second half,' he said. 'See you.'

Back in the sitting room the teams were out on the pitch again. Candia had stopped even pretending to take an interest and was reading a copy of *Possession*. Suddenly Alexandra heard Douglas say, 'Good God, it's Tom!'

'What is?'

There was a copy of *Time Out* balanced on the lip of a magazine rack. Douglas seized it and threw it on the floor beneath the TV. 'That is. That's Tom.'

Looking at the upturned face, with its flat, regular features and garnish of fashionably short hair, Alexandra remembered being somewhere in Oxford, some party full of the dreadful people you saw at parties of that kind, people who acted in plays or worked on the magazines. People like her, she reflected uncomfortably.

'I thought you knew about Tom,' Alain said.

'I heard he was in films or something, but…'

'Oh, he's made it big all right.'

There was a roar from the screen. Alexandra watched the ball ballooning high off an outstretched leg and career into the net as a back-pedalling goalkeeper tried hopelessly to retrieve it.

'Fuck,' Douglas said. 'Fuck, fuck, fuck.' She knew, though, that half of him wasn't thinking about the football, was still, in fact, considering the question of Tom and Hollywood and a contract worth – Alexandra could dimly remember a story in the *Standard* now she thought about it – worth however many millions of dollars it was.

'That was some deflection,' Alain said authoritatively. 'Came off Parker.'

'What a wanker that bloke was,' Douglas said. 'I mean, do you remember him in tutorials? It was a miracle he ever got there in the first place. And then in finals – you're not going to believe this, Alex – we came out of the Political Thought paper, someone asked him about one of the set books, and it turned out he hadn't read *Leviathan*. Didn't even know what it was.'

'He used to go out with that Westmacott girl, didn't he?' Alexandra asked.

Douglas was doing fairly well, she thought, to pass all this off as amused exasperation or exasperated amusement. Watching him as he looked at Alain, who stared back rather worriedly, she could see he was making a conspicuous effort to control himself.

'A date with Helen Westmacott? They used to call her ex-boyfriends the potholing and mountaineering club.'

'Don't think me rude or anything,' said Candia from the sofa, 'but will you stop going on about Tom. Only he happens to be rather a friend of mine.'

'A friend of *yours?*'

'That's right. A friend of mine. So will you please stop going on about him?'

'Candy...' Alain began.

'Hey,' Douglas said. Alexandra still couldn't tell whether he was seriously angry, or still humorously exasperated. 'I grew up with Tom Newsome. And I think I can say whether he's a wanker or not.'

'I think growing up's putting it a bit charitably, don't you?' Candia said. 'Look, let's put it another way. Will you please stop laying down the law on things you know hardly anything about? We had Mrs Thatcher at supper. Now it's Tom Newsome. I suppose after this stupid football match it'll be government fiscal policy or something.'

There was another bellow from the screen. 'Lineker,' Alain said anxiously. 'Equaliser.'

Alexandra stared wonderingly around the room: at Douglas, who was silently opening and closing his mouth; Alain, half turned to the TV screen; Candia, who had gone white in the face and was drumming her fingers against the cover of her book. 'I'm sorry,' she said. 'You're going to have to excuse me.'

They watched her go. On the screen the white figures danced, re-grouped, broke apart.

'Ex-boyfriend,' Alain said. 'Sorry. Should have told you.'

'Even so.'

'Even so. Exactly.'

'One all,' Alain said after a while. 'Anything could happen.'

Much later – at one or two in the morning – they went to bed in a high, oak-panelled room looking out over the inky lawn. 'I'm so disappointed,' Douglas kept saying, as he tossed his clothes item by item onto the bedside table. 'Bloody Pearce, just hacking it like that. I mean, what do we pay them for?' Looking at him as he lurked at the foot of the bed, ribcage gleaming in the sharp light, shirt tugged over his head, Alexandra thought that he wasn't in the least moved. Something else struck her about the low, sluggish rhythm of the day and she said:

'Why didn't you tell me Macmillans had turned your book down?'

He blinked for a second, weighing up his response. 'Because it doesn't matter. Someone else will take it. It just doesn't matter.'

It would always be like this, Alexandra supposed: her watching him summon the strength to cast off these rebuffs, forever standing there flushed, irritated but finally invulnerable. She twisted slightly in the bed as he slumped down beside her, thinking for some reason of Gary Nichols' farmboy grin, her nineteen-year-old self stepping timorously through the college quadrangles. 'I'm so disappointed,' Douglas muttered again into the pillow at her side.

'So am I,' she said.

—1998

Rainy
Season

'And then there's that occluded front heading in from Finisterre,' the man from the Meteorological Office finished up. 'Should reach the Dorset coast in the morning.'

'That's good to know,' Alex said. He had made a resolution quite early on in the job not to be intimidated by jargon. 'What effect will that have?'

'Same as usual, I should think.' Alex admired the man from the Meteorological Office's expertise, but he could sometimes be worryingly non-committal. 'Nothing you could lay a bet on.'

Beyond the window the sky was darkening over, bringing a faint, depressive chill to the rows of computer screens and the knot of crop-haired girls busy at the photocopier. Putting down the phone, Alex wrote *rain in the South?* on a yellow Post-it note stamped with the TV company's logo, which somebody had once said reminded them of an SS officer's shoulder-flash. He was a youngish man with a prematurely bald head and a pink-and-white complexion who had read several books by Richard Dawkins and believed fervently in the eventual triumph of scientific rationalism. Until that time came he was researching for the lunchtime show. Sometimes these were the best jobs in television. But not always. As he put down the phone Belvedere, who was the programme's economic correspondent and could occasionally be seen in the newspaper room reading the business page of the *Daily Mail*, stopped at his desk and said: 'Did you see Eurydice's live report on the north-east hurricane?' 'No. What happened?' 'Knocked down by a freak wave on Scarborough front. You never saw anything like it.' 'That's bad,' Alex said. He supposed that some deep-seated melancholic flaw in his temperament had brought him to the weather bureau. His dreams were always of surging black clouds, beach-huts smashed to matchwood by triumphant surf, interminable molten rain. One of the crop-haired girls bent to retrieve a packet of paper-clips, and the movement of her wrist reminded him of Erica who, he realised with a spasm of unease, he had forgotten to phone.

Shortly afterwards Mr Stafford called a meeting in his office and they all crowded in: Leanne who did the lighting; Agnetha, who replied to readers' emails about what their barometers were saying; and the girl whose name no-one could remember who sometimes burst into tears in the wash-room. Alex sat in the rickety chair by the filing cabinet, inconspicuous, but difficult wholly to ignore. That was the way. Mr Stafford was an animated man in his forties who was thought to have ambitions to direct a game show. Just now he was working in current affairs and liked interfering with the autocue ten minutes before transmission. He said: 'I know you think I don't take any interest in the weather. But I do. I expect some of you saw the latest set of figures. Let me tell you they make pretty grim reading. I'm afraid Euridyce wants to go back to children's television. She says it's safer. Does anyone have anything to say?'

'I don't know if you saw,' Alex volunteered, with practised diffidence, 'but we had a new graphic last week. That rolling thunderbolt with the black border. It was rather good, I thought.'

'Yes, I did notice it. It didn't do anything for me. In fact, I saw something very similar on Channel Four only the other day.' Alex remembered that Mr Stafford, unlike most members of his profession, watched television in the evening. There was no accounting for taste. Outside the rain rattled ominously on the window. He wondered if Erica had got anything for supper, and whether she expected him to deal with the leaking radiator in the bedroom. You could never tell with Erica.

Mr Stafford was still talking about the figures. Alex thought about the million absconding viewers who switched off after the news. He imagined them priming kettles, buttering toast, tearing the rings from cans of beer, anything to avoid their responsibilities. Mr Stafford said: 'I think we're all agreed then that it's a question of viewer identification. I can't say I'd have chosen Natalia Spendlove myself, but the people upstairs seem to like her and apparently she's at a loose end since that cookery show got taken off the air.' Alex tried to remember whether Natalia Spendlove was the one who had been in the papers founding the animal sanctuary in Morocco or the one who had ended the career of a parliamentary under-secretary. Sometimes it was hard to keep up. 'Any comments?' Mr Stafford asked. He had bumpy, luminous skin that looked as if it had been grafted from an expensive handbag. 'Isn't she a bit odd?' Alex wondered. 'Odd?' Mr Stafford turned the word over on his tongue. 'I suppose you might call her odd. Doesn't she belong to some weird religion or something?' But all religions were weird, Alex thought, trapped for a moment in the meeting's death-throes, the people caught half-in and half-out of their seats, the light bouncing off the protrusions of Mr Stafford's face, the girl who sometimes burst into tears in the wash-room drifting brokenly towards the doorway. Science; foresight; the rational interpretation of verifiable fact: that was what would save us.

Back at his desk a new tranche of data had appeared on the screen, and he silently appraised it, relishing its calm exactitude, its spatial distinctions. In Uttoxeter it was raining. Fog, coalescing over the East Anglian coast, was moving in towards Great Yarmouth, Cromer and King's Lynn. Heavy showers tracked across the Medway. People too, he thought, had this susceptibility to analysis, this potential for enslavement to the grand laws of pattern and design. All that was needed was confidence in one's judgment. As the lunch-hour passed, waiting for Erica's 1.30 phone call, he read *The God Delusion* with what he hoped was an appropriately serious expression. 'I won't be back until late,' Erica said, ringing at 2.15, 'but if you get home by six it would be a big help as the man's coming to see about the radiator.' 'I thought I was going to fix the radiator,' Alex said. 'Did I? I must have forgotten. Bye, darling.' Putting down the phone, Alex found himself obscurely irritated, as if twenty square miles of storm cloud heading north across Lincolnshire had suddenly changed course and gone off to inundate the Midland plain. Belvedere, ambling past the desk with a copy of *Tax Tips for the Over Sixty-Fives* in the nicotine-stained fingers of his left hand, whistled sharply and said: 'Natalia Spendlove, eh?' 'What's that supposed to mean?' Alex wondered. It was not that he wanted to fix the radiator, he decided, merely that he required certainty in his life. 'Oh come *on,*' Belvedere said. The shrug of his shoulders implied war, famine, pestilence, cataracts descending out of an azure sky. Suddenly Alex wanted solidarity, something to set against the vagaries of a capricious world. 'Where are you going?' he asked. 'Interview some bleeding cabinet minister about the budget,' Belvedere said. He went off briskly down the corridor, the noise of his footfalls moving in counterpoint to the tap of the rain on the glass.

Slowly – infinitely slowly – the remainder of the week passed. There was no sign of the radiator repair man and Alex did the job himself: a bucket full of treacly water, weighed down with sediment, sat on the kitchen floor in tribute. Rain fell in the Peak District, the Scottish Borders and the Brecon Beacons, and Belvedere was reprimanded by his editor for not having heard of the International Monetary Fund. The vague thought of trouble that Alex now detected in his life – an ominous foreshadowing, a presentiment of doom – was compounded by the arrival of Natalia Spendlove. He had supposed that Ms Spendlove – such was the immemorial habit of weather presenters – would have bountiful, wheaten hair, white, even teeth and be dressed in something by Nicole Farhi or Paul Smith. Instead, bidden to the hospitality room where she sat awaiting her induction, he found a small, sullen girl with a dyed black buzz-cut wearing a white boiler-suit with odd floral attachments that made her look rather like a

Morris-dancer. 'Might as well be banging a couple of staves together on Chiswick Green,' he complained to Erica, during one of the discussions they were having – he in his flat, she on a mobile somewhere in Kensington High Street – about where they might go on holiday. 'Shall I book the tickets, then, for Andalusia?' 'Spain's rather hot,' Erica objected. 'You said you liked it last year when you went to Oporto.' 'A girl likes a change sometimes,' Erica said, her voice suddenly overwhelmed by the snarl of traffic.

In the end Mr Stafford vetoed Natalia's boiler-suit, and they compromised on a business outfit in white pin-stripe. The problem about the job he did, Alex thought as she laboured over the screenful of new computer graphics that Mr Stafford wanted for Natalia's inaugural spot, was that it furnished an endless series of metaphors for the rest of your life. You saw your relationships in terms of warm fronts and suspect cloud-gatherings, your past as a chain of isobars rising and falling on the grid. Wondering, in spite of himself, how he and Erica shaped up on the meteorological chart, he decided that after a period of occasional showers and the odd thunderstorm they were moving forward to a more settled climate. The computer graphics glared back at him from the screen – flaring sun-bursts, grey chevrons cunningly engineered to give an impression of continuous deluge. He rang Erica at the flat, where she had professed to be working that afternoon, but there was no answer. The long-range forecast said that there were thunderstorms across Newfoundland, Greenland and the western Atlantic, and he logged the data happily on his chart. Those Newfoundlanders and Greenlanders would just have to look out for themselves. 'Here,' Belvedere said, walking past. 'Guess what I saw that Natalia Spendlove reading in the foyer just now?' 'I really have no idea,' Alex said. He had begun to wonder whether Belvedere was a serious person. 'Book of *Exodus*,' Belvedere said.

On the day of Natalia Spendlove's debut there were gales across north-west England and the Marches. 'Force nine in Llanfair Talhaiarn,' the man from the Meteorological Office said cheerfully. 'You might want to issue some kind of alert.' 'I thought you said it was going to be mild for the time of the year?' Alex queried, remembering a conversation from the previous day. 'Did I? Well, it's very variable. Strong winds and an area of high pressure. Difficult to predict.' Alex could see the email that had come that morning winking from the screen. He was taking her for granted, Erica wrote. She would send a bike round tomorrow for the keys. Here were other things that were variable, beyond the weather. He wrote a little précis of the man from the Meteorological Office's remarks and circulated them to the department. Everywhere he looked, he thought, the fixed, immovable pillars of his life were crumbling into dust.

'I really don't see that there's anything for me to apologise for,' Mr Stafford said, when they assembled next morning. 'In fact there was some very positive viewer reaction. One can't expect everyone to appreciate this sort of thing instantly.' He did not look as if he had slept, and the skin of his face was shinier than ever. Presently the telephone rang and they all filed out while he decided whether to answer it. 'The best bit,' Belvedere said, as they loitered by the coffee machine in the mournful forenoon, 'was when she started shouting about plagues of locusts.' 'And Noah,' Alex said, judiciously. 'The bit about Noah was good.' 'They've already fixed Stafford's replacement,' Belvedere went on. He was smiling because he had just been promoted to full business editor. 'That old chap from the gardening spot.' Later, staring at his computer screen, Alex remembered the shrewd, maniacal look on Natalia's face as she had pronounced her incantations. Somewhere along the way he had lost his faith, he told himself, that austere, modernist belief in order, destiny, the consolations of a rational life. There was a storm heading in across the Suffolk coast, and he thought about the people in the Southwold beach-huts, hunkered down beneath the spirals of vibrating air, felt, for the first time, a twinge of rapt, vicarious terror.

—2008

Passage
Migrants

C ome mid-August the light in Sheringham began to change. In the past it had hung in duck-egg blues and greys over the warm summer sand. Now it had turned gun-metal: cloudy even when there was no cloud. Morris watched it again that morning as he stood in the big, untidy room that looked out on to the beach, pulling a hand uncertainly over the three days of stubble on his chin. On the couch, a yard or two distant from the high windows, snug under blankets and Morris's old parka jacket, the girl from the Marine Ballroom slept soundly on, orange hair thrown back over a makeshift pillow of supermarket bags.

It was about half-past eight. Outside there were terns massed on the sandbar: two hundred of them at least, Morris calculated. Further out, beyond the upturned boats and the wreck of a giant sandcastle built three days before, gulls skirmished over the breakers. Once, at dusk on a day such as this, Morris had seen what he assumed was a purple heron rooting through driftwood in the shallows, but for some reason the hastily palmed camera had realised only vague shapes of grey and cobalt, the bird itself gathered up and lost in shadow. Thinking of the heron made him remember the figure on the couch. Morris hadn't meant to come home with the girl from the Marine Ballroom. To find her there eight hours later, pinched face white against the black cushions, was to register a troubling shift in routine, like setting out along the coast path on the cliff to find it strewn with granite blocks from the sea defences.

Traipsing along the sea front on his way to get a paper – the door slammed sharply behind him by way of a hint – Morris watched the tern armies huddled against the breeze. In an hour or so they would head north to the flats at Cley or Brancaster. He walked back the way he had come, noting other routines that were undisturbed: fishermen hauling crab boats over the shale; an ice-cream van being restocked from a delivery truck; dog-walkers silhouetted against the shoreline. Back at the flat he found the girl from the Marine Ballroom sitting at the big deal table wearing one of his old tee-shirts and eating slices of unbuttered toast.

This bread must be a week old,' she said. 'Look, it's got green bits growing out of it.'

Her hair was redder then he'd thought, Morris realised: a kind of scarlet orange with magenta tints. Seeing it bobbing above the table-top nonplussed him. It was outside his range. There was a rucksack he hadn't noticed yet, half-open on the floor and spilling books and tissues out over the sandy hardboard.

'Nice place you've got here,' the girl went on. 'Apart from the cafeteria.'

Morris reckoned she must be a year or two younger than himself: twenty-two maybe, or twenty-three. He lingered for a moment by the window, gently lashing the sill with the furled copy of the *Cromer Mercury*, meditating another hint.

'Where are you staying?'

'The Beeches. Out on the Holt Road. I don't suppose you know how to get there?'

Morris nodded. Everyone in Sheringham knew about The Beeches. On Friday nights Range Rovers drove out from Norwich, Cambridge – even as far as London – dropping off gangs of moneyed teenagers at the gate. Two years ago there had been a scandal when a girl drowned in the swimming pool. Still rapping the sill with the newspaper, he gave directions. Beyond the window the sky threatened rain.

'I've to go to work,' he said, casting out the final hint.

'That's OK. I'll let myself out.'

Morris left her there among the mouldy bread-crusts, the stacked crockery and the copies of *Norfolk Bird Club Bulletin*. Looking up at the window a moment or two later, as the flock of terns swept northward over his head, he could see her moving beyond the glass: a ball of orange flame bleeding into the nondescript greys and fawns behind. Down at the marina they were gearing up for the late-summer rush. Mr Silverton thought the season would last another fortnight. Then the schools would go back and the trippers start to disappear. Morris sold ice- cream, mended a catch that had come off one of the fun-pool cubicles and retrieved a Walkman that someone had dropped into the deep end. At the mid-morning break he and Doug, the other assistant, sat and smoked cigarettes on upturned crates in the yard, hunched against the tubs of chlorine and the rusty generator spares, while Mr Silverton came down from the upstairs office and took a turn at the front desk. Outside fine rain fell against the Perspex dividing wall and they could see the shapes of the holidaymakers clustered against the big overhanging sign that said SHERINGHAM'S NEWEST INDOOR AQUATIC EXPERIENCE.

Curiously, the girl – her name was Alice, he now remembered – was there again at lunchtime. From his eyrie above the soft drinks dispenser, where the wiring had begun to come away from the wall, he noticed her turning over the rubbish in the bargain swimwear trays that Mr Silverton bought in job lots on the back of Norwich market: nonchalantly, but with an undisguised sense of purpose. When she saw him she came over and stood by the dispenser, waiting for him to descend.

'Does it always rain like this? In this part of the world, I mean.'

Out of the corner of his eye he could see Doug regarding him sardonically from the desk. 'Pretty much.'

'Do you get a lunch break?'

'It's another half an hour.'

Waiting in the foyer while he sold tickets to a cub pack superintended by two mountainous Akelas, she looked oddly out of place, Morris thought, like one of the birds you saw at the big reserves further up the coast: blown off course, not sure what the food was like or whether the natives were friendly. They had a ploughman's in one of the pubs along the front, in a small room hemmed in by fishing nets and ancient lobster shells. Alice was a student, taking a year out between degrees. Mostly she lived at her parents' house in London, but there was talk of Edinburgh, Exeter, places even further flung. There were other people from The Beeches in the pub: two girls in striped men's shirts and sunglasses and a boy carrying a copy of A *History of Western Philosophy.* At intervals their mobile phones went off, and they fished unselfconsciously in bags and pockets to answer them. Bored with the conversation, Morris stared out over the beach and its flotsam: marauding bands of children, an old man in an antique bathing dress tottering gamely towards the sea. 'There's a party on Wednesday at the house,' Alice said, when he got up to go. Why don't you come along?' 'I'll do that,' Morris said. Wednesday was the day he worked late.

Back at the marina he found Mr Silverton cross-legged on the floor beside the ice-cream cabinet, surrounded by a pile of melting choc-ices and sky-ray lollies, trying to mend an electrical fault. He was a plumpish, middle-aged man with thick, brindled hair like a badger, whom Morris and Doug had christened 'The Fatman'. 'There's a bloke in the foyer wants to know about a party booking for the Bank Holiday,' he said, without looking up. 'You'd better go and talk to him.' Heading off to reception, Morris found that Alice's pale parched face, the flock of terns on the beach, had mysteriously coalesced in his head, so much so as to displace the other things that burned there.

The afternoon wore on. Mr Silverton finished repairing the ice-cream cabinet and went off to do errands in town.

'What happens here in winter?' Morris wondered over their tea-break.

Doug, who lived down the coast at Cromer, nodded at the imputation of local expertise. 'You ever been here in November Morrie boy? Half the shops shut down. Fatman takes six weeks in Torremolinos. Day a week maintenance for the likes of us, if we're lucky.'

155

Though we would never dream of interfering, Morris's sister Julie had written a couple of days before from her house in Slough, *Gary and I feel it is time you faced up to your responsibilities.* It all depended on what your responsibilities were, Morris thought. He had a memory of walking through the front door in Slough a year before and Gary instantly asking him to wipe his feet. There was a fifty pence piece lying on the scuffed lino beneath the reception desk, and he picked it up and put it in the till.

'Soft bugger, you are,' Doug said, without malice. Outside an ice-cream van's klaxon rose like an air-raid warning over the silent streets.

Late summer came. Waking up in the flat, Morris could feel the time slipping away, like sand from the high dunes falling out of his hands, down to the distant beach. Alice had left a paperback novel behind her on the couch: puzzling, unrecognisable spoor, about a group of girls sharing a flat in Bayswater. Morris examined it a couple of times before he handed it back. There was nothing in it that he could fasten on, still less any clue to Alice. In the evenings they went exploring the empty Norfolk back-lanes to Holt, Happisburgh and Burnham Market. Here there were unexpected surprises: two blind men playing chess in a cafe near Wells; an artist in a graveyard near Gresham busily transforming the church into a terrifying surrealist skyscraper; an older world, turned in on itself, inviolate. Julie wrote again, gossip and warnings jumbled together. The children were doing well at school. His mother was ill. There was a bed for him whenever he wanted it. On the Bank Holiday it rained for seven hours. Mr Silverton sat at the reception desk ostentatiously leafing his way through travel agents' brochures. Doug had disappeared, gone off to Norwich or working at Yarmouth funfair: nobody quite knew. Julie's letters lay face-up on the deal table, covered with beer can ring-pulls and postcards of Sheringham seafront. 'Do you ever write back?' Alice wondered, putting a pack of groceries down on the floor. She had taken to buying him things, Morris registered: bags of sugar; men's magazines; Mars bars. There was a soft, proprietorial air to the way she moved round the flat. 'What are you doing at the weekend?' he asked, on a whim. 'Nothing.' 'There's somewhere we could go,' he explained. 'Somewhere I haven't shown you.' 'OK,' Alice said. 'I like surprises.' Morris could see that she was intrigued, that it was the right thing to have done.

'Next week,' Alice said, as they sped out on the coast road that Sunday, 'I shall have to be getting back. Really and truly.' Morris nodded, hoping that this would absolve him from speech. There were teal flying alongside the car, a long line of them heading north to the Wash. The sanctuary at Titchwell was just as he remembered it: a pinewood shop selling bird books and pairs of binoculars, elderly men in waders and soft felt hats drinking coffee out of thermos flasks in the yard. On the sheet of card tacked to the wall there were details of the passage migrants: stone curlews, avocets, an osprey that had flown in that morning with a Swedish ring tag round one of its claws. Later they wandered off along the path to the sea, past the twitchers' hides and the observation points. The light had gone grey again, Morris saw, turning the sky the colour of the filing cabinets in Mr Silverton's office.

What was that?' Alice wondered, tugging suddenly at his sleeve. Morris felt rather than saw the blur of movement at his feet – like a brightly coloured paper bag, he thought later, lofted skywards by the wind. Watching it come to rest, a dozen yards down the path, orange crest bobbing above the dark wings, he felt a surge of exhilaration. 'It's a hoopoe,' he said. 'Look! I never saw one before.' There was a file of middle-aged women in mackintoshes coming along the path towards them. Boxed in, the hoopoe took flight again, westward over the salt marshes. Morris watched it go. Not long after it began to rain again and they retired to the car. 'That festival I was telling you about in Devon,' Alice said briskly. 'Once I've parked my stuff in town I'm off down there. You ought to come.'

Morris stared through the streaming window as the birdwatchers' cars manoeuvred through the mud. The hoopoe would be somewhere over the north sea now, far away from the cam-corders and the binocular arcs, out where he couldn't follow. 'Sorry,' he said, seeing the beach in winter, snow on the breakers, blanketing the rock pools in soft white fur. 'Things to do.'

—2001

Birthday
Lunch

The Terrapin Club was finally run to earth in the northernmost quadrant of Covent Garden, stuck between a unisex hairdresser and a shop that sold filing cabinets. Even then there was a difficulty, as the staircases ran both up and down, with only a Post-it-note-sized notice stamped TERRAPIN CLUB: MEMBERS ONLY to show the way. In the dining room a waiter in a white coat stood polishing a tray of tumblers, and a radio played Mantovani's 'The Song from the Moulin Rouge'. Mr Brancaster sat at the far end, fat white hand curved solicitously around a wineglass. When he saw Patrick he raised his forefinger up to the level of his temple and gave a mock-salute.

'You're three minutes late,' he said, 'so I took the liberty of ordering a drink.' Mr Brancaster was a stickler for seemly cliché. He was the kind of man who partook of spirituous refreshment and availed himself of public transport. At some point in the past he had enjoyed marital relations, and Patrick was there to prove it.

'Meeting with a client,' Patrick told him, stowing his briefcase beneath the table. 'Couldn't get away.'

'It matters not,' Mr Brancaster said, loftily. He had never taken any interest in his children's jobs. Chartered accountancy; estate management; rat-catching: it was all the same to him. Snapping his fingers, with a noise that broke the room's silence as effectively as a dropped brick or a banshee's wail, he exclaimed: 'Waiter! *Garçon! Jugend!* Another glass of the wine that maketh glad the heart of man, *if* you please.'

It seemed that the waiter was used to Mr Brancaster's foibles. He brought a glass of wine on a brass salver, so tiny that it might have been an ashtray, and then went back to burnishing his tumblers. There was still no one else in the room.

'Who are the Terrapins?' Patrick asked, taking a sip of the wine and regretting the partners' dining room in Eastcheap. He had a vision of a shoal of miniature tortoises quietly manoeuvring their way up the rickety staircase. 'Do they ever show themselves?'

'Of course they show themselves,' Mr Brancaster said. He was quiet for a moment and then went on: 'The chairman of the wine committee is a Cinq Port baron.'

They had been having these birthday lunches for a dozen years: in carvery restaurants in the shadow of Holborn Viaduct; in pasta joints on the south side of Oxford Street; and now in the Terrapin Club. It was hard to know if this was a step up, or a retreat.

'You're looking well,' Patrick said. It was a quarter past one. He would stay until 2.30, but no later.

'I am well. My leech, never yet suspected of being a humbug, says he has never seen a fitter man of seventy-nine.' As well as seemly cliché, Mr Brancaster liked professional archaisms. He was probably the last man in England to talk about barristers-at-law and water-bailiffs. Sappy, damson-faced and vigorous, white hair combed back from his forehead, blue-blazered and pink-shirted, he looked like a Butlin's redcoat or the kind of old-fashioned comedian who strode up and down a line of chorus girls singing 'Dapper Dan was a very handy man'.

'And how's Marjorie?'

Marjorie, as the younger generation of Brancasters never failed to remind each other, was dangerous territory. Without Marjorie there would have been no birthday lunches on neutral ground, and no Mrs Brancaster, still furious at her desertion, mouldering in the divorcée's bungalow at Firle. But Mr Brancaster took this in his stride.

'She keeps me young,' he said, with what to anyone else might have been a glimmer of irony, but which Patrick knew to be absolute seriousness.

There were three or four other Terrapins in the dining room by now: innocuous-looking men in sober suits, who peered respectfully at the wine list and the framed photograph of the Duke of Windsor drinking a cocktail and looking as if he had just stepped in something nasty. A door in the corner opened and shut suddenly and the smell it released – mingled scents of cabbage, gravy and burnt sugar – was so like Patrick's school canteen that he raised his head from the table and sniffed at it. Mr Brancaster, meanwhile, had summoned the waiter again ('Waiter! *Garçon! Jugend!*') and was putting on a tremendous performance – a really first-class show, even for him – about the lunch menu. Like the stink of the cabbage, this, too, brought back memories: of Mr Brancaster at school open days; at football matches; in saloon bars and on petrol station forecourts. No one, Patrick thought, had ever made such an exhibition of himself or failed to notice that an exhibition was being made.

'It's a pity the two of you don't come and see us more often,' he said, when the waiter had been sent scurrying away. 'Marjorie's often said so.'

But not even kind, tolerant Elaine could be persuaded to visit the house in Pinner where Mr Brancaster sat in state watching antiques programmes on the television more than once a year. 'It's not for me to complain,' she had once said, 'but people who go around deliberately ruining other people's lives ought to be called to account every now and again.'

'It's a long way on a Sunday afternoon,' he found himself saying, 'and besides, the children have their own lives to lead these days.' That was another effect that time spent in Mr Brancaster's company had on you: he encouraged you to spout the same evasive language as himself. In fact there was no earthly reason why Patrick's children could not have been forced to visit their grandfather on Sunday afternoons, other than their not liking him. For Mr Brancaster was an insensitive grandparent, who made bracing remarks about exam results, twitted the boys about non-existent girlfriends and, worse, could not see the damage he was doing. Looking at his father as he sat comfortably in his chair, the white hair so immaculately angled over his scalp that it might have been made of spun sugar – Marjorie was twenty years his junior – Patrick wondered, not for the first time, what he had wanted out of life. To be a success? Well, that depended on how you defined success. To be loved? Well, a fair number of people had, at one time or another, loved, admired, or at any rate tolerated him during the course of that seventy-nine years. No, he decided, what Mr Brancaster had really wanted to do, and showed every sign of continuing to want to do, was to impress his personality on the world around him.

'I hope it's not one of those days where the chef pretends he's feeling under the weather,' Mr Brancaster said, a bit too loudly for comfort. 'I once had to go into the kitchen and grill the sardines myself.'

They were never any good, these birthday lunches, whether at the Holborn carveries, the Soho pasta joints or anywhere else. They were never any good because their effect was to focus attention on the past: a past in which Mr Brancaster, though conspicuous, would always be found wanting. Had he ever, Patrick wondered, made an original remark? Had he ever got beyond that fervently held first principle of pleasing yourself? And this was to ignore the spectre of Marjorie, which hung over everything the younger Brancasters had done, said, or plotted, in the past ten years like a giant bat. 'It's very *hard*,' Mrs Brancaster had said, rather humbly and matter-of-factly, when the fact of Marjorie's existence had first been drawn to her attention. There was no getting away from this, none. It was hard. And Mr Brancaster had made it harder still. It was not, Patrick thought, that you could excuse the things he did – had done – would continue to do – on grounds of increasing age. After all, you accepted that your parents' behaviour would become more stylised as they grew older. Even his mother had adopted a high-pitched little-girl-lost voice and was keener than ever to talk about some quasi-aristocratic relatives whom they barely knew. It was just that his father's behaviour – whether young, middle aged, or grandly decaying – had always been exactly the same.

'*Cyril! Kenneth! Derek!*' Mr Brancaster was calling out greetings to the other Terrapins, who stirred uncomfortably in the breeze of his salutations, like anguished dreamers. There was something terrifying about his bonhomie, Patrick thought, terrifying and somehow meaningless.

'Happy birthday, dad,' he said, remembering why he was there, still guilty despite all the evidence piled up in his favour.

'Better than some,' Mr Brancaster said. 'Do you know there was a time in the RAF when they tried to serve me up with a plate of celery?'

The food began to arrive and they ate it: potted shrimps, which Mr Brancaster gnashed into fragments, like a lawnmower tearing up twigs; some bread rolls, which he tweaked out of their basket with his finger-ends and laid, one by one, on his plate like an oysterman displaying his catch. And then something odd happened. Caught in the wash of Mr Brancaster's personality, and either anxious either to conciliate it or simply make some half-ironic comment, the waiter set down the next course – an outsize chunk of cod garnished with mange-tout – with what, in the context of the Terrapin Club, its dingy backdrops and dust-strewn carpet, amounted to a flourish. Something in the gesture struck home at Mr Brancaster. He said, suddenly and unselfconsciously:

'This reminds me of the fish.'

'Which fish?' Patrick asked.

'The fish. You, of all people, ought to remember the fish.'

Mr Brancaster had always been a high-grade exponent of private codes, crosswords solved by clues that only he had access to. This must be another one of them.

'I remember all kinds of fish,' Patrick said, a bit irritably. It was ten to two now: soon he would be gone.

'No, the fish we caught that time at Happisburgh. On the beach. When the sea had gone out. And then we took it home and your mother cooked it.'

And, curiously enough, against all expectation, he did remember. Slowly, like a priceless carpet, the scene rolled out to fill his head. Long leagues of unmarked sand. The sea a distant, blue-white line. A commotion in a rock-pool, which turned out to be not, as they first thought, a cat but a three-pound cod left stranded by the departing tide. His father expertly despatching it with a rock-end to the head. He would have been seven, he supposed.

'I do remember it,' he said.

'I knew you would,' Mr Brancaster said. Vindicated, he grew quieter, less self-assertive. It would have been possible, had Patrick thought any of these things desirable, to borrow money from him, tell him a few home truths, even pass on a message from his wife. Outside the window the noise of Covent Garden boiled up from the street. A kind of calm settled on the proceedings. 'All a long time ago,' Mr Brancaster said, like a headmaster deciding for once to lay the imposition book aside. 'Didn't your mother say – didn't she say it was the maddest thing I'd done in a long while?'

'I expect she did,' Patrick said. His mother, he remembered, had made the best of things, put her supper-plans aside and boiled up the cod in pint of milk.

'All a long time ago,' Mr Brancaster repeated, upping the level of his voice to a resonant, head-hunter's chant.

After a while more food came, and Mr Brancaster attacked it with the same attritional fury. Patrick sat silent in his chair, his own meal untouched, oblivious to the Terrapins and their modest chatter, lost in this world of rolling sand, his father's taut, eager, face, that blissful anaesthetic of endless skies, yachts dancing in the distance, time, for once, stood still, waiting for him to do whatever he wanted with it, and make it whole.

—2011

Cranked Up
Really High

B eyond the kitchen door the lawn descended into sunlight. Coming from twenty feet away still deep within the house, the fat man's voice – was his name Roger? Or Jeremy? – seemed curiously disembodied, hanging in the air above the trails of Virginia creeper and the outsize plant pots.

'Of course there are things we ought to have done to the place, I don't deny... But when it comes down to it, I mean, in the end you've got to *live* in a house haven't you?'

Ignoring the voice, to the extent that its brisk, man-to-man bark was ignorable, Julian stared critically across the grass. A hundred feet, perhaps, or a hundred and twenty. Where the lawn ended there was a cluster of miniature outbuildings: two sheds, a ramshackle summerhouse, what looked like a compost heap trammelled behind wooden bars.

The voice was drawing nearer again. Close up it seemed less substantial, somehow ghost-ridden. 'As to the garden, there's a bit of a stench first thing in the morning. Down-wind of the local pig farm, I'm afraid. But if you want to live in the country, then really that's the kind of thing that...'

Turning back on his heel Julian watched the fat man come lumbering through the doorway two coffee mugs sunk into the red flesh of his fists, half-smoked cheroot still dangling from the fingers of his right hand. The fat man's name, he now remembered – and this kind of confusion was endemic to serial house inspection – was Hugo. Despite the open-necked shirt and the bare, plump feet crammed into espadrilles, the adjective that suggested itself was 'soldierly'. You could visualise Hugo in battledress commanding the prow of a tank, giving orders to Gurkha riflemen.

They set off across the lawn – Hugo determinedly, as if he was shouldering his way through bracken – past an apple tree and an oak bench lightly dusted with powdery green lichen. Here the small, red-haired girl that Hugo had shooed briskly out of the hall when they arrived was sitting with a pile of windfalls in her lap. Hugo's expression, which had been proprietorial in the dining room and bored in the kitchen, now registered simple annoyance.

'I don't think,' he said solemnly, 'that we want any of *that*.'

'Sorry, daddy.'

'You know you're not supposed to eat the windfalls, darling. Now, go and put them in the box in the scullery so that mummy knows where they are.'

'All right.'

'Otherwise there won't be any to make into preserve, will there?'

'I suppose there won't.'

Julian watched the girl skidding back across the grass, apples gathered in the crooked knot of her arms. Hugo was looking at the cluster of outbuildings, momentarily baffled, like an actor robbed of a vital cue. Then his face brightened.

'Now, if you're a gardening man, well, here's something that really, I mean…'

The something turned out to be a motorised lawn-mower with a defective rotor blade that Hugo proposed to 'throw in with the house'. Standing by the doorway of the shed, in the shade of the mighty cypress trees that bordered the fence ('Cost you three hundred a year to trim, of course, but there's a chap two doors down who, I mean...') Julian wondered, as he usually did on these real estate tours, what Hugo did for a living. Even with people called Hugo, who lived in moss-covered rectories out in the Norfolk wild, it was sometimes difficult to tell. There had been a mass of sailing charts strewn over the deal table in the study, but that didn't prove anything. Remembering the black stuff gown that meek-eyed Mrs Hugo had been commanded to carry away out of the lobby along with other weekend detritus, he marked him down as a barrister.

'Good solid pinewood, that fence,' Hugo chipped in, taking this moment of reflection as waning interest. 'So if you wanted to prune back the hedge, you could...'

Two months into the search for a house Julian was familiar with this kind of language: the language of uplift, exhortation, limitless possibility. Rock gardens just waiting to be turned into swimming pools. Dowdy attics craving the coat of paint that would transform them into playrooms, studies and guest annexes. Somewhere in this world of ritualised embellishment, moral obligation lurked.

'Any particular reason why you're selling?' he wondered as they trekked back uphill over the scree of windfalls. Hugo, looking slightly more affronted than most vendors allowed themselves to be by questions of this sort, muttered something about schools, wives and proximity to work. It was eleven in the morning now, and hot. Looking up at the house (a *highly desirable rectory conversion on the edge of this much-loved village*) he saw his own wife silhouetted against one of the upstairs windows, the agents' brochure fanned out beneath her gaze. Mary would be half-way through her check-list by now: roof; drains; village school's position in the OFSTED table; bus service; danger of flooding; local burglary statistics; neighbours. Curiously, people answered these questions with an unfailing patience. The protocols and assumptions of house purchase – common ground, inches offered and received – appealed to them. Watching Mary bob her head in answer to some response from Mrs Hugo – invisible behind curtains – reminded him that starker realities lay at hand. 'If we don't get this one,' she had said in the car earlier that morning, hand poised over the mobile phone in her lap, 'it'll mean another six-month let. Five thousand out of the capital. Just think about it.'

Julian thought about it, as they wandered back inside. Hugo was staring suspiciously at the corpse of a gigantic slug that lay suppurating on the mat. 'Bloody cats,' he pronounced. 'They just bring every bit of wildlife they can find indoors, and, I mean, it's not as if…' Julian wondered if he left his sentences unfinished in court. 'Last week I found a dead *weasel* on the landing,' Hugo went on. From the tail of his eye Julian saw the red-haired girl issuing secretively through the hall and heading towards the staircase. 'Look,' said Hugo. Julian saw that he had straightened up from the mat and resumed the demeanour of someone who seriously wants to sell his house. 'This is rather fun.'

Julian examined the miniature pulley system suspended above their heads, from which various hooks and wires hung down.

'What does it do?'

'What does it do? Well, you stick something on one of these hooks – like this, see? – and then you just, I mean…'

Some way above, footsteps could be heard moving over an uncarpeted floor. With elephantine precision Hugo put an ashtray onto the wire cradle and sent it chugging over to the other side of the ceiling. Julian had a sudden vision of him as a serious-minded boy unpacking train sets, whisking toy cars round their circles of track. 'I'd very much like to see upstairs,' he said, 'see if Mary's come up with anything.' 'Actually,' Hugo riposted, flipping the ashtray neatly out of its cage, 'we'll probably be taking this with us, that and the, I mean…' By degrees, and by way of an inspection of the scullery damp course, they beat a path back to the dining room, where there was a sideboard supporting decanters and a line of family photographs: a younger Hugo with slightly longer hair in rugby kit; Mr and Mrs Hugo on their wedding day; a recent Hugo staring peevishly at something feathery and dead sticking out of a Labrador's muzzle. Beyond the door, at the foot of the staircase, the red-haired girl was sitting on the bottom-most step crooning softly to herself and plucking clothes pegs one by one out of a vermilion bag.

'Darling. Annabel. Darling. We've had this conversation before.'

'What conversation daddy?'

'The conversation about not leaving things on the staircase. About what would happen if anyone fell over them.'

'Yes.'

Halfway along the upstairs landing, dwarfed by a giant
representation of some Monet waterlilies, Mary and Mrs
Hugo were huddled over a sheaf of architect's drawings. As
he approached to greet them Julian thought he heard the
words 'extension over the garage roof'. Seeing her husband,
Mrs Hugo announced, not without all signs of trepidation,
'They want to see the loft.'

The *loft?*'

That's right, you see...'

'No. That's fine. That's absolutely fine. Darling. I'll just
get the, I mean, and they can...'

Unhooked by means of a long silver pole, the loft trap-door
fell open. Further tugging realised a patent ladder that Hugo
managed to unfurl to within an inch or two of the carpet.
Silently they clambered up, the small red-haired girl leading
the way. It was a spacious loft, Julian divined, the best they had
seen: fifty feet long, boarded, with storage cupboards, and
capable of fulfilling his solitary criterion for house purchase,
which was a study-cum-bookroom. They hovered about for
a moment while Mary got out her tape measure and Julian
tried not to notice, or to be seen to have noticed, that one
of the books in the pile of paperbacks spilled over the floor
was called *High Jinks in a Women's Prison*. Hugo, he saw, was
looking pleased, like some schoolteacher whose most back-
ward pupil has, against all odds, managed to recite a poem
or conjugate a French verb.

'What's behind this curtain?' Mary wondered. She gestured in the direction of a kind of tarpaulin slung over one of the furthermost beams.

'That?' Hugo looked affronted again. 'Some nonsense of Annabel's. I don't know. Actually, though, there's a lot more space there than, I mean, perhaps we ought to...'

'Daddy, it's not nonsense.' Julian saw that the red-haired girl had suddenly materialised beside them, at once hugely animated and bitterly upset.

'Darling. Daddy is trying to show Mr and Mrs... Mr and Mrs... and really...'

'Daddy, you mustn't let them see.' There was something quite desperate in the girl's face, Julian saw: lost, worn-out, end-of-tether.

'Hugo...'

'No, darling, really don't see why I can't...' Hugo was calling back over his shoulder as he foraged through the heaped-up boxes. What followed Julian remembered only as a tableau of noise and colour: Hugo's beetroot face, dust motes hanging in the bright air, the surprisingly loud slither that the tarpaulin made as it hit the floor, the pink, glassy faces of the rows of dolls revealed behind it; the whole perfectly unsinister apart from Annabel's banshee wail as she threw herself forward in their defence.

Back in the car ('Some bloody nonsense, no idea why she, carrying on like that, I mean...' Hugo had confided on the journey downstairs) they drove through back lanes crowded out with loosestrife and cow parsley. 'Well?' Mary said expectantly. What did you think?'

'Not terribly exciting,' he said, keeping it non-committal despite his fury. 'What about you?' 'Dream house. Just ravishing. Apparently he's been made redundant, so they're desperate to sell. And Mrs Warren says they'd let us have eight off for the state of the roof.'

Julian thought about Hugo being made redundant, the pink face growing steadily pinker as sentence was pronounced. 'Well, we're not buying it.' He was quite surprised at the sound of his voice, the memory of the small girl's face suddenly streaking into tears. 'Not if it was the last house in Norfolk.'

There was silence for a moment. Signposts flicked by to Holkham and Wells-next-the-Sea. 'You're cranked up pretty high aren't you? Mary wondered in faint bewilderment. It was an old, pet phrase they had, from years back, denoting sudden access of emotion, loss of temper.

'I'm sorry,' he said. 'Really, I am.'

That night, while Mary slept in front of the rented TV, he wrote out the cheque to the letting agency. Later, in his dreams, the red-haired girl ran on blithely over endless tropical dunes while, far below on the beach, Hugo lay up to his shoulders in sand as the apes, capering with glee, threw ripe fruit at his head. There were ways of behaving, he thought, whole worlds that existed beyond the arc of red-faced barristers and their silent wives, sides that needed to be taken, even here amid the crawling ivy and the distant, shimmering lawns.

—2002

Wonderland

Here in December the view beyond the lecture room had taken a turn for the worse. Like most scenery, it was less than reliable. Late afternoon made the overhang of trees by the lakeside ominous; the lake itself downright sinister. There were no students about. They were in junior common rooms, on buses heading townward, into their varied recreations, out of their heads. On the other hand the orange lights – luminous and Belisha Beacon-like – bobbing about in the darkness suggested that someone had taken a boat out into the lake's northward reach. This was odd, as boating was forbidden, along with swimming and kayaking. Definitely odd, she thought, as she raised her head from the page of lecture notes – to be honest, a sheet of Basildon Bond writing paper with the words *Eliot, tradition & individual talent* and *epiphany* scribbled on it in failing pencil – and, gripping the sides of the lectern with a greater firmness than she had previously allowed herself, told the class that what Virginia Woolf had really brought to the English novel when it came down to it was a mythologisation of the processes of ordinary life.

As soon as the sentence was out of her mouth she knew she had made a dreadful mistake, but there was no going back. The class stared at her: not with hostility, but blankly, like a double row of moon calves. They were all there, or nearly all of them. Girls mostly. (A couple of sarcastic boys sometimes sat at the sides asking questions calculated to fox her.) There was the frail, anorexic one who had once fainted from hunger during a lecture on Gertrude Stein. The fat-arsed one, whose mother or whose boyfriend or whose back-line buddy in the lacrosse team ought to have been told to tell her that skin-tight jeans above two-tone pixie boots were a thoroughly bad idea if you weighed one hundred and eighty pounds. The dull, sisterly pair who sat together in the very middle of the front row and had never, in the course of a dozen lectures and a real-live fire alarm, said a word either to each other or to anyone else. And then, squashed into the right flank of the back row, the planes of her face so flattened that she might have been pressed against a pane of glass – not a politically incorrect observation, Amy thought, for this was exactly how she looked – *Mikado* hair-do wilting a little in the heat, Miss Chen, Lily Chen, formerly of the University of Taipei or some such, who, of all the students who had ever waltzed into Amy's class on mid-period modernism, was the one she most wished to throw out into the street on a charge of false pretences.

The Belisha Beacon was still bobbing in the prow of the boat and there was a scrabbling noise as a boy with ridiculous dreadlocked hair put his head tentatively round the door-frame, saw that he had come to the wrong room and then unapologetically withdrew. Two miles away in his office Giles would be writing some press release, or emailing the chairman of the Kidderminster Conservative Association. A hundred and twenty miles away in the antiques shop in Camden Sam would be doing – well, what exactly would Sam be doing, except what he always did, which was – let us be realistic about these things – to break his parents' heart?

'I expect you can think of other modernist writers to whom this mythologising was an essential part of their engagement with form,' she heard herself saying – brightly, but not so brightly as to introduce an element of pastiche. In fact, Amy had no such expectation, but these days you were supposed to involve them in what were sometimes rather grandly called the potentialities of discourse. Joyce. Eliot. Mansfield. The famous names rattled on, like stones in a tin can. As the lecture hall clock inched forward to five, her audience stirred perceptibly. The race had run its course. The fire had burned down. It was at this moment, at this part of the day, and at this stage in the term that Amy always wanted to throw her notes away and yell: *Give up this world. It will do you no good. Return to the lands you came from. Live humbly and put not your trust in academe.* But that way madness lay. Some of the overseas students were paying £13,000 for the privilege of hearing what she thought about the early poems of Sacheverell Sitwell. A colleague in the department of Creative Writing had once got into serious hot water for telling her students that the discipline they practised was so institutionalised as to effectively constitute a branch of the Civil Service.

The bobbing, boat-borne lantern had disappeared now, possibly to the part of the lake that lay out of sight behind the porter's lodge and the approach to the sports hall. One of the sarcastic boys was rolling a cigarette. Lard-arse was stuffing her roly-poly fingers into a pair of mittens. Lily Chen texted heroically on. Amy brought her hands smartly together, like a supplicating nun in a medieval frieze, concluded her address with the words 'benchmark of modernism's assimilation into the literary mainstream of the inter-war era', waited politely to see if anyone wanted to talk to her – there were no takers – and then stalked out into the over-heated, brightly illuminated third floor corridor of Arts Block Three, home of English Literature, Romance Languages, Viking Studies and, somewhat incongruously, Experimental Psychology.

There was relief here, but also uncertainty. The way home led along this third floor corridor of Arts Block Three, next to which the other two Arts Blocks now reared unignorably up, but it also led past a number of departmental noticeboards, any one of which might harbour some unwelcome piece of news guaranteed to stall her progress. And, most calamitously of all, it also led her past the office of her immediate superior, Graham Jamieson, Professor Graham Jamieson M.A. (Oxon), PhD (Warks), 'GBJ' of the inter-departmental memo and known to the junior staff as 'Sound of marching footsteps' owing to his habit of appearing to be in continuous transit along the university's myriad corridors, its concreted walkways, its greenly landscaped cross-campus tracks, at precisely the time you most wanted to avoid him. He was bearing down on her now, clearly making for his office, but equally clearly making for it at a pace that would enable him to be two yards short by the time she reached the door.

'Hello Amy. I didn't know you came in on Wednesdays.'

'Well I do,' Amy said, wanting to add *You plan the bloody timetables, Graham, so perhaps you ought to,* but in the end merely smiling in what she hoped was a respectful manner. She had never known how to deal with Jamieson. Junior lecturers tended to conceptualise the university on Harry Potter lines. Students were Muggles. The Vice-Chancellor's office was the Ministry of Magic. Of Jamieson it had several times been said that he had gone over to the Death Eaters. He was also supposed to know the name of the Vice-Chancellor's wife's Siamese cat.

'Teaching your modernism class, I expect.'

'That's right,' Amy said, wanting to add: *see what I mean about planning the bloody timetables?* The overhead lighting gave the faces that passed beneath it a washed out quality, and made Jamieson's look like a piece of cold boiled veal. He had short, stubby fingers, curiously whorled with dirt, as if he had spent the past few hours burrowing far underground.

'Many there?'

'Not too bad,' Amy said, the vision of the veal still haunting her, as well as one or two other childhood phantasms she could have done without, and then, quite unable to resist the temptation: 'Even Lily Chen turned up.'

In the context of Amy's relations with Jamieson, this was a step too far. On the other hand, the angle of his body – slumped half-way into his office, one hand pressed against the laminated notice that read *Professor Graham Jamieson, English* – suggested that he had already decided to shanghai her inside.

'Actually I think that's a tiny bit harsh,' Jamieson proffered, in his neutral, head-of-department's tone, which made a change from his matey, we're-all-in-this-together tone, but was perhaps more sinister. They were standing in his office now, next to the photograph of him shaking hands with Stephen Fry and a bookshelf on which reposed no fewer than 17 hardback copies of his *Hardy's Poetics*, of which the *Times Literary Supplement* had remarked that it was 'in every sense jejune'. 'I looked up Lily – Miss Chen's – attendance record only the other week, and really it compares very well with some of the other students.'

'Not, of course,' Amy said, 'that we're allowed to mark them down if they don't turn up.'

'Do you know, Amy,' Jamieson said, pretending, and failing, to be delighted by this remark, and at the same time making an arch out of his fingers, like a small child who has just produced a church and intends to go on and construct a steeple, 'there are times when I don't think you like your students very much.'

'It's not that,' Amy said, thinking that the smile on Stephen Fry's face as he was being introduced to the proud author of *Hardy's Poetics* could not possibly be genuine. The room, with its powerful scent of Jamieson's personality – there was even a picture of Mrs Jamieson, Clementine she might have been called, in full hill-walking, up-and-down-daleing fig – had begun to oppress her. She wanted to be back in her own world, however devitalising, with its news of the Kidderminster Conservatives and whatever nonsense Sam had sent back from Camden Town. 'It's not that she turns up to one seminar in three, or spends the whole time texting when she is there. I dare say I would have done the same at her age, given the chance. It's just that she can barely speak English and hasn't read any of the books she's supposed to be studying.' *And that somebody with full knowledge of her accomplishments let her in in the first place,* she wanted to add.

From outside in the darkness came the sound of an ambulance hurtling in the direction of the lake. The smile on Stephen Fry's face was definitely a sneer, she decided. He had seen through Jamieson and despised him.

'And then there's her coursework,' she concluded, thinking that Jamieson could not make her stay in his office beyond 5.15 p.m. on a Wednesday in December, that she had fulfilled all expectations that could be reasonably held of her, and that she was going to walk out of it whether he liked it or not.

'Oh yes,' Jamieson said, with what for him was considerable suavity. 'I'd rather like to discuss that with you, seeing that we've had the second examiner's report. Perhaps you could come and see me in the morning? I'd say now, but the M.A. people have invited a couple of sound poets to come and talk to them and I really ought to be there. Shall we say 10?'

They said 10. The ambulance siren was still wailing, but the noise of the engine had stopped. Here in his sanctum, surrounded by his paraphernalia – the back numbers of the *Journal of Coleridge Studies* and the collected works of John Cowper Powys – Jamieson's face looked less palely ascetic. Perhaps he had some kind of a romantic life. You could never tell. She strode off towards the end of the corridor, down two flights of stairs, out through the breeze-blocked foyer and into the dimly lit stairwell where, eight hours previously, she had chained up her bicycle. It was still in one piece, except that someone had plastered a flyer advertising an LGBT conference slantways across the seat. In the semi-darkness the air was raw and smoky, blown in across the wide East Anglian plain. Eastward, beyond the sports park and the crazed outlines of the dental school, pallid lights winked from the council estates. There would be trouble about Lily Chen's paper on T.S. Eliot's classicism, trouble about the paltry forty-nine marks that Amy, after much soul-searching and not a little annoyance, had ended up awarding it; trouble, and then, once she had taken aboard whatever Jamieson had to say about it tomorrow morning, more trouble. Usually the bicycle was her solace, the quinquereme in which she sailed quasi-majestically down the hill and then up the short slip-road that brought her home, but there was no pleasure in it now, not when all she wanted was news of her menfolk, Giles and Sam, the first of whom had, some years ago, mysteriously lost what was supposed to be the safest Conservative seat in the whole of the West Midlands, and the second of whom had said goodbye – there was no way of getting round this, no possible means of glozing over what had happened – to his reason.

Back at the house there were lights on in hall and kitchen, and a hedgehog lying dead – no doubt symbolically – in the drive. Inside the front door the dog, a debased and rickety dachshund, was toying with some potato peelings it had rooted out of the supposedly unbreachable compost bin and Giles was standing by the telephone, receiver in hand, attending to what sounded like a recorded message playing back. An arctic chill swept out of the drawing room, and she went to adjust the thermostat, noting as she did so that several other early Christmas cards had appeared on the pile on the sideboard and that one of them was from the Prime Minister and his wife.

'The people at Kidderminster called half an hour ago,' Giles said, coming into the kitchen where she stood eating a banana, with the card – rather a dull one with a picture of Downing Street in the snow still clutched between her fingers. 'Didn't even make the shortlist.'

'That's a shame,' she said, the *best wishes from David and Samantha* searing into the flesh of her palm. 'Who did they go for?'

'Anstruther. The Badger. Wimbledon-Smith. The one whose name I can never remember with the prosthetic leg.' A travelling caravan of aspiring Tory MPs toured the safe seats, always leaving one of their number behind on the morning they broke camp. But Giles's place at the caravanserai grew ever more precarious. He was fifty three now, a decade and a half older than the Badger and Wimbledon-Smith.

'I shall really have to start thinking seriously about giving this up,' Giles said haplessly. She liked him much more now that he was no longer in parliament, and there were fewer crackpot phone-callers. 'There's a message from Sam on the machine.'

The doorways of the house – sitting room, dining room, kitchen, downstairs loo – gaped at her. 'What sort of message?

'Listen for yourself.'

She put the Christmas card back on the pile and, milk-white face with its high, grey-brown halo of hair looming towards her in the hall mirror, switched on the answerphone. Sam never called anyone's mobile. As his rigmaroles went, it was far from unprecedented; comforting even, in that it went no further than distances previously covered. The snow-bound tundra might be gleaming out there beyond the circle of firelight, but the wolves had been kept at bay. While she listened she thought of the moment – irrevocably fixed in her mind – when she had decided that Sam was different from other children, and that a substantial part of her life would be given over to exploring that difference and sanding down its edges. It had happened when he was about three years old and she had come upon him sitting on a sofa, cat gathered up in his arms – that he had liked the cat had always been a point in his favour – watching some children's programme or other, and appreciated – on what evidence she could not quite say – that the look on his face was more than simple intentness, or fixity or vision, that, like some of the outwardly innocuous remarks let fall by Professor Jamieson in his office, it meant trouble. And now there he was, sixteen years later, working in an antiques shop in Camden and living, or not living – nobody was sure about this – with the woman who owned it and leaving bewildering and ironical and sometimes transparently furious messages on the answerphone.

'I don't think he sounded quite as bad as last time,' Giles said when she had finished, coming out of the kitchen with a bottle of wine – the last of the bottles his constituency association had given him on his defeat – in the slender fingers of his left hand.

'What does he do all day in that shop?' Amy demanded, not so much of Giles, who had begun to tug hopefully at the bottle with a corkscrew, but of the world at large, that great unseen audience which lurked silently in the dark garden and thronged the ceiling above her head. 'Does he read books or dust the chairs? And Tamsin, or whatever her name is, what does she do all day? Hold his bloody hand? Read his Tarot cards?'

There was no answer to this. Later on rain fell and she went out into the drive, torch in hand, and, with water dripping onto her head from the leylandii hedge, set about burying the hedgehog.

The big news on campus next morning was of the student drowned in the lake. This, then, was the explanation of the bobbing lantern and the ambulance churning up mud as it sped to the water's edge. More shocking even than the death, Amy thought, was the manner of its accomplishment. For the girl who had decided to end her life had simply walked into the water wearing a trenchcoat whose pockets were full of rocks taken from the Vice-Chancellor's ornamental garden, like Virginia Woolf consigning herself to the currents of the Ouse. Here on the third floor of Arts Block Three the view from Professor Jamieson's window was full of authenticating detail. There was still a boat out cruising the windblown surface of the lake; the landing stage where walkers threw sticks for their dogs was already carpeted with flowers.

It was about half past ten and the overhead lighting was more unflattering to the faces of the people beneath it than ever. Outside in the corridor students were queueing to receive end-of-semester grades, lobby for coursework extensions, unburden themselves of feelings of unworthiness, guilt and despair. Did universities have a beneficial effect on the people who studied at them, and the people who supervised them? Was there, when it came to it, anywhere else for them to go? These were not questions that would ever have occurred to Professor Jamieson, who had several copies of Lily Chen's coursework strewn over his desk and was looking at them with unfeigned enthusiasm.

'As you know, Amy,' he was saying, in what she thought was a surprisingly good imitation of dispassionate neutrality, 'we have a series of procedures that are brought into play should it turn out that two examiners disagree. Or, that is, if they disagree to such an extent that the whole basis of the undertaking is called into question.'

'I take it that means the whole basis of the undertaking has been called into question?'

'I think so,' Jamieson said, with irreproachable seriousness. 'Yes, I definitely think so. If you had given Lily – Miss Chen – let us say a fifty three or even a fifty two, perhaps one could let it stand. But a forty nine… That, I think, is really impossible to ignore.'

In the antiques shop in Camden Town Sam would be staring out of the window at the fine North London rain. Or would he? The problem with Sam was that he so rarely did what anyone else did. The stock response to the stock situation was completely beyond him. He was far more likely to be hurling Frisbees on Primrose Hill. With an effort she returned herself to the business at hand.

'The reason I gave her a forty nine, Graham, is that she can hardly write English. I mean, I take it that students on the twentieth-century course are expected to make subjects agree with verbs?'

Jamieson raised both his hands to the level of his chin, in what was presumably intended as a gesture of self-deprecation but ended up looking merely odd. In the distance, by the lake's edge, she could see a little drift of students, altogether dwarfed by the immensity of shrub and foliage, come to examine the floral tributes.

'Why don't we step back from this a moment, Amy, and look at the situation from Miss Chen's point of view? Certainly, we have a right to expect our students to write in grammatical English. On the other hand, there is the question of the support that we, as an academic institution, owe to them. Now, I must say that having met Miss Chen in the course of my administrative duties I have always found her to be articulate and indeed enthused by her studies.'

Heads of department had to say these things. All their geese were necessarily swans. Were they any students anywhere, Amy wondered, who were dim-witted, uninterested and unable, or unwilling, to read the books? Forty years ago one of Jamieson's predecessors on the faculty had written a semi-famous novel, supposedly set within the confines of Arts Block Three. Advertised as a campus romp, it was, she had always thought, a rather melancholy book, whose subterranean thesis was that the values supposedly trumpeted by universities were all too prey to subversion, that liberalism, when you came down to it, or when you established it in Arts Block Three, had its price.

'Let me ask you a question, Graham,' she said. 'Is anyone here ever allowed to fail anybody?'

But Professor Jamieson was too old a hand to be fooled by this kind of ploy.

'I had hoped,' he said wearily, 'that we could have resolved this. Clearly we cannot. Miss Chen, I may say, has submitted a formal complaint alleging bias. She also claims that you made an insensitive and belittling remark with reference to something she had written about E.M. Forster.'

'All I said was that if she was going to write about Forster's novels, she might at least get the titles right.'

'Has it never occurred to you, Amy, that the Miss Chens of this world – any student, if it comes to that – need careful handling?'

'When I was at Oxford,' Amy said incautiously, 'the Miss Chens of this world would have been given six penal collections and then sent down.'

After that it was agreed that there was no point in going on. They arranged to meet two days later in the offices of the Dean, where the whole question of Miss Chen's coursework and, by implication, Amy's fitness to judge it could be gone into at greater length. Having established that the matter was out of Jamieson's hands, Amy cheered up.

'Graham,' she said. 'Have you ever read *Wonderland*?'

'You've got me there. Is that a new one?' Contemporary literature was a closed book to Professor Jamieson.

'The novel by Martin Cartwright. The one set here.'

'Oh that. No, I don't think I have.'

'You ought to read it,' Amy said, greatly daring. 'It would tell you something about yourself.'

'Ah, literature,' Jamieson said, who had his whimsical side. 'So often thought to be heuristic. So rarely up to delivering the goods.'

Afterwards, cycling back down the hill into a vicious wind blown south from Jutland, she could not quite work out why she needed to make a principle out of Lily Chen. There had been other Lily Chens over the years, and she had let them go: a boy, once, who had done no work for three years, and with whom she had remained on the friendliest possible terms; a girl who had copied page after page out of Terry Eagleton's *After Theory* and been let off with the mildest of cautions. Why should they be allowed to prosper and Miss Chen sink into the icy depths? Reaching home at twelve to discover that Giles had gone to his office and that the dog had been sick on the floor of the utility room, she was gripped by a sudden access of resolve, as painful and unsettling as a tumble into a nettle-bed. She would abandon the afternoon's marking, go up to London on the train and roust out Sam from his antiques shop. No sooner had the idea formed in her head than all the disadvantages that attended trips to London clamoured to supplant it, but she fought them off, cleaned up the dog sick, left a note on the kitchen table for Giles, which said simply, but, she thought, rather enigmatically I HAVE GONE TO LONDON and then stepped smartly outside before she could have second thoughts and caught a bus into the city. It was growing colder, and the people in the streets had that dull, exasperated look so characteristic of the East Anglian winter. Quite often, going up to London on the train, there was someone else she knew, some colleague traipsing up to deliver a paper, some mother of a child from one of the several schools Sam had attended in the vicinity until the educational process grew weary of him. This time, ominously enough, her carriage was almost empty and she spent the journey staring out of the window at the dun-coloured meadows and the pools of stagnant water that ran away on either side of the track, anonymous and alone.

Camden, when she reached it, seemed even nastier and more untidy than on her last visit, and the schoolchildren gathered in the entrance to the Underground station like creatures from another galaxy. What did they want? And what was to be done with them when they grew older? She had a vision of two of them walled up behind glass in some foreign museum under the rubric *specimens of English youth, London, December 2012*. The antiques shop proved not to be down the side street where she thought she remembered it, but at the far end of a tiny, sequestered square where so many black refuse sacks lay piled up in mounds that they could not possibly have all belonged to the buildings round about and must have been brought in from outside. The twilight was coming on now, and a part of her did not want to go into the shop, feared what she might find there, would have given anything, in fact, to have been able to jump into a taxi and have herself driven back to Liverpool Street, to have left the moral dilemmas which oppressed her to the characters of the books on which she lectured. On the other hand, was there any guarantee that the authors of these works knew any more than she did? She took her hands out of her coat pockets, stared into the shop window – depthless and atmospheric – and was rather relieved to find Sam sitting on a stool next to a pile of dinner plates and an ostrich egg on which the plump faces of their majesties King Edward VII and Queen Alexandra had been blandly superimposed: less disconcerting-looking than usual, she thought, but with a bizarre hairstyle, cropped to the skull on one side but with queer, luxuriant fronds hanging down on the other. When he saw her he got down off the stool and stood awkwardly with his hands by his sides, rather if, she thought, he was a boy scout waiting to be called to attention, and she was struck by how unutterably incongruous her life had become, that you could live for nearly five decades, cultivate the most sophisticated opinions about art, taste and morality, have a complete set of the Scott Moncrieff Proust at your bedside to comfort you, and end up married to a Conservative MP who had lost his seat and staring in the dim interior of a shop called Alice's Attic, wondering if your only son, who looked as if he had been half scalped, would deign to speak to you.

'I thought I'd come and see you,' she volunteered. 'I was just standing in the kitchen at home, without very much to do, and I thought I'd get on the train and come and see you.'

'That's nice,' Sam said. Some of the clumps of hair at the back of his head had been dyed an unlikely shade of blue, she saw.

'Where's Tamsin?' she asked, thinking that if Tamsin had appeared in the shop she would happily have thrown the ostrich egg at her.

'Gone to a sale in Palmers Green, I think.'

A customer coming into the shop might have relieved some of the awkwardness, but Alice's Attic did not seem to run to customers.

'Sam,' she said, not untruthfully, 'whatever you might think of me, it's very nice to see you. But I haven't had anything to eat or drink since this morning, so would you please make me a cup of tea?'

Later on, when she thought about it – travelling back on a train full of tetchy commuters and then in the skidding taxi – she realised that in the context of her recent dealings with Sam, it had not gone altogether badly, that he had not, as had sometimes happened in the past, talked arrant nonsense, that he had listened to her questions and returned answers that were broadly coherent, that on a scale of ten an informed judge would probably have awarded the conversation six or even seven. On the other hand, as she discovered when they sat eating supper in view of the dark, cheerless garden, it was difficult to explain exactly what part of the encounter she had found encouraging.

'How did he seem?' Giles wondered tentatively. He was much less emphatic these days.

'I don't know. How does anyone seem? He was quite chatty – for Sam. He's had his hair cut in some weird new way.'

'And is he actually living with… Tania, is it?'

'Tamsin. It would be a very odd set-up if he weren't… *Jesus*,' Amy said suddenly, the mountain of reasonableness she had built up for herself over the past three hours instantaneously collapsing into runnels of sand. 'He's twenty. He ought to be at college somewhere, not working in an antiques shop with some raddled old hippy chick who looks like something out of the Incredible String Band.'

'Do you think we ought to tell Tony?' Tony was, or had been, Sam's psychiatrist.

'It can't do any good. But yes, we probably ought to.'

Two other significant things happened that evening. The first was that she found the Prime Minister's Christmas card torn up and flung in the waste-paper basket – flung, she thought, with a kind of ostentation that could only have meant that the flinging was a message to her. The second was that she went up to the book-room and looked out a copy of *Wonderland* in an old Penguin edition with a florid inscription – *To darling Amy with fondest love from James* – on the title-page (and who was James? She could not even remember) and spent the next hour or so skimming through its parched and curiously friable pages. The reading of it came as a shock to her – not because, as she had dimly anticipated, it was a much more ground-down affair than the jaunty encomia of the back jacket led you to believe, but because the people at large in it – the randy academics, the guileless women they were bent on seducing – were so entirely different from anyone she had ever met. They were not innocent people, and they were not neutral – they were Marxists, and Feminists and Materialists

and (a few of the older ones, anyway) Existentialists, and sometimes devious with it, but there was a kind of Romanticism
about their efforts to preserve a tiny, uncontaminated corner
of the academic world where, untroubled by questions of
profit and loss, they could attempt to be themselves. On the
other hand, Amy thought, if there was one thing that nearly
three decades of adult life had taught her, inside a university
and beyond it, it was that you should be deeply suspicious
of Romanticism.

Cycling up the hill to the university for the meeting with the
Dean, past grey, Titanic lorries that loomed up unexpectedly
from out of the mist, she found that there was a paragraph
forming in her head which could be used not exactly in her
defence but as a way of assimilating the events of the past
few days, in so far as they could be assimilated. It went: *all
this, all the endeavours on which we are so optimistically engaged,
are effectively meaningless. If Miss Chen, against whom I have no
personal animus, is allowed to come here and buy a degree, without
having the ability to read, much less comprehend, the books she is
supposed to be studying, then why shouldn't anyone? As for the idea
that what we do here has any relevance to the world beyond the window
of Arts Block Three, that literature, as it is currently taught, is an
ameliorating force, that it is a source of moral rejuvenation, that it
encourages us to see ourselves in perspective – that it possesses all
those wonderful sanctifying qualities we are constantly told about –
then let me tell you that the experiences of the past week suggest that
literature has no bearing on whether I feel happy, sad or anything*

else, and certainly no effect on my ability to cope with the impediments that life strews in my path. She thought that this was putting it rather strong, but never, she realised, had she felt keener on putting things strongly.

In the end all this, all this unabashed cultural extremism, went unsaid. For the Dean's office turned out to be empty, its door open, its complete edition of the *New Oxford Dictionary of National Biography* laid out invitingly in its double row, but the long sofa on which supplicants were invited to state their cases quite empty, and the birds flown – if, indeed, they had ever perched there in the first place. She had been there ten minutes and had time to read a whole article about Stefan Zweig in the *London Review of Books* when there came a shuffling noise in the doorway and she looked up to see the burly, chronically put-upon figure of Dorothy, the Dean's secretary.

'Are you waiting for Maurice and Graham? I'm afraid neither of them's here.'

'Why not?' Amy demanded, more petulantly than she meant to. 'Why aren't they here?'

'Actually,' Dorothy said, coming into the room and shutting the door with an adroitness that belied her all-in-wrestler's physique, 'they're with the V-C.' There was a pause. 'I think they'll probably be there most of the morning.'

Amy cocked an eye. This was too big to be ignored. Much bigger than the Registrar being arrested in the nightclub or the cannabis patch in the woods. Happily Dorothy was an old friend. They had shared bottles of water after the charity fun run and criticised many an outfit worn by the Public Orator's wife. After she had made a pretence of tidying the Dean's pristine desk and returned the copy of the *London Review of Books* to its proper place, she said:

'Actually it's a disciplinary matter.'

'To do with whom?'

'Professor Jamieson.'

'What's he done?'

There was a pause while Dorothy searched for the appropriate quasi-legal phrase. 'Apparently he is supposed to have forced his attentions on one of the overseas students.'

'Anyone we know?'

'I believe,' Dorothy said, indicating both that the conversation was at and end and that Amy could consider herself lucky to be divulged even this much, 'that she's called Lily Chen.'

Lily Chen, Amy thought, Lily Chen! What havoc have you wreaked in the breast of occidental man since you first flew in from the University of Taipei, or wherever it was? Such unprecedented news demanded a response, and so she left the Dean's office, in all its anti-septic splendour, and marched off to the cafeteria in the shopping mall which occupied the campus's central square in search of a cup of coffee. Outside the foyer they were holding a vigil for the girl who had drowned herself in the lake, and there were students standing about in groups holding placards which said REMEMBER VIOLET. All this, too, seemed incongruous. Nobody was called Violet these days, nobody, and somehow the placards seemed to emphasise her detachment from the world and the forces that had led her to do away with herself. But all this was serious, Amy thought. Whatever Jamieson had got up to, or perhaps only contemplated, with Lily Chen was squalid, or offensive or laughable, but there was no getting away from the placards. When the university reassembled after the Christmas vacation somebody, she knew, would have created a shrine by the water's edge with pictures of Violet laminated at the campus coffee shop and doggerel poems written by people who had known her.

Drinking her coffee and looking out over the square, she wished that she could separate the critical apparatus she brought to her professional life from the world that extended beyond it. The people who wrote those poems for Violet – if they did write them – would be doing so with the best intentions. The last thing they needed was some bright, merciless intelligence criticising their scansion. There were not many things she envied in her son, but one of them, she thought, was the ability to live your life as it happened, without the eternal critic, that metaphorical F.R. Leavis or John Carey perched on your shoulder. Just as she was thinking that Lily Chen's inadequacies were probably not, or not entirely, Lily Chen's fault, that vast external forces that Lily Chen had no way of resisting had probably brought her here on this magic carpet ride from the mysterious East, she realised that the girl sitting ten yards away behind the copy of *Closer* was, as a certain part of her consciousness had already hinted to her, indeed Lily Chen. Lily Chen, whose knowledge of the Bloomsbury Group was as full of holes as a Jarlsberg cheese, but who had in some grotesque and unfortunate way apparently been pawed over by Graham Jamieson. You could not, Amy decided, deny someone the moral support they needed because of their ignorance of Virginia Woolf. You could not even deny it because you disliked them, or you suspected that they disliked you. In her mind she was back in the shop in the Camden square, where fierce old faces looked out of the frames of Victorian paintings, trying, and, as she suspected, failing to say the right thing, not even sure that the right thing could be said. Was there a right thing to be said here? Who knew? Coffee cup rattling in its saucer, the copy of *Closer* flapping before her like some ancient guerdon rallying a troop of medieval soldiery on their hill, she moved hesitantly, but hopefully, forward, in search of some elemental solidarity that had once existed in her life but had since gone missing from it, that ancient wonderland where moral feeling was simply moral feeling, babies lay uncontaminated in their cradles, and lakeland water flowed on undisturbed.

—2014

Acknowledgements

Of the stories included here, 'Jermyn Street' was first published in Nicholas Royle, ed. *Neon Lit: Time Out Book of New Writing 2* (1999). 'As Long as He Lies Perfectly Still' appeared in the *Independent on Sunday*. 'Charcoal' was published in the *Sunday Express Magazine*. 'Wrote for Luck' was broadcast on BBC Radio Four and appeared in the *Literary Review*. 'Teenyweeny Little World' and 'Blow-ins' were broadcast on BBC Radio Four and appeared in the *Eastern Daily Press*. 'The Disappointed' was published in Nicholas Royle, ed. *The Agony and the Ecstasy: Short Stories and New Writing in Celebration of the World Cup* (1998). 'Rainy Season' was broadcast on BBC Radio Four. 'Passage Migrants' was broadcast on BBC Radio Four and appeared in *Pretext*. 'Birthday Lunch' was published in *S* magazine. 'Cranked Up Really High' appeared in the *Mail on Sunday's You* magazine.

I should like to acknowledge the help and encouragement of the various editors and producers who originally commissioned or accepted these stories, in particular Nicholas Royle, Suzi Feay, Christie Hickman, Nancy Sladek, Trevor Heaton, Ali Smith and Julia Bell. Especial thanks are due to Sam Jordison, Eloise Millar and Henry Layte, without whose kind invitation this collection would not have existed.

D.J. TAYLOR is the author of eleven novels, including *English Settlement* (1996), which won a Grinzane Cavour prize, *Trespass* (1998) and *Derby Day* (2011), both long-listed for the Man Booker Prize, *Kept: a Victorian Mystery* (2006), a *Publishers' Weekly* book of the year and *The Windsor Faction* (2013), joint winner of the Sidewise Award for Alternate History. His non-fiction includes *After the War: The Novel and England Since 1945* (1993), *Thackeray* (1999) and *Orwell: The Life*, which won the 2003 Whitbread Prize for biography. He lives in Norwich with his wife, the novelist Rachel Hore, and their three sons.